# THE RABBIT HOLE MURDERS

## WONDERLAND DETECTIVE AGENCY BOOK 2

JEANNIE WYCHERLEY

The Rabbit Hole Murders:
Wonderland Detective Agency Book 2
by

JEANNIE WYCHERLEY

Copyright © 2021 Jeannie Wycherley
Bark at the Moon Books
All rights reserved

Sign up for Jeannie's newsletter: https://www.
subscribepage.com/JeannieWycherleyWonky
*The Rabbit Hole Murders* was edited by Christine L Baker
Cover design by Ravenborn Covers
Formatting by Pink Elephant Designs
Proofing by Johnny Bon Bon

Please note: This book is set in England in the United Kingdom. It uses British English spellings and idioms.

CHAPTER 1

"Mm-mm-mm," I mumbled, channelling my inner Oliver Hardy and swiping at the corner of my mouth to stop myself from drooling in public. I had my nose pressed against the steamy windows of Betty's Bakery, like some starving street urchin. I was trying—valiantly, I thought—to choose from the array of cakes on display but kept changing my mind.

The beauty of living and working in Tumble Town, I'd found, was that there were little pockets of joy among all the darkness, devilry and misery. Betty's was one of these. Whereas most bakeries open early morning and close mid-afternoon, Betty's remained open until late in the evening and never seemed to run out of hot pies and pasties, sausage rolls, sandwiches or cakes. This had, at times, proved detrimental to my wallet, but today, Wonderland's very own office assistant, Wootton Fitzpaine, turned the grand old age of twenty-two and I had promised to treat everybody.

'Everybody' amounted to three humans, namely myself, Wootton and Hattie, who owned the building and ran The Hat and Dashery, her hat shop on the ground floor. But I couldn't forget Snitch, full name Bartholomew Rich, who had been my first client and had become a professional hanger-on ever since leaving Witchity Grubbs—otherwise known as Her Majesty's Prison Witchwood Scrubbs—around six weeks previously.

Our non-human resident was DS Ezra Izax, my partner while I'd been working for the Ministry of Witches Police Department. The gruff but knowledge-able detective, with his silvery hair, wiry eyebrows and heart of gold, had come to mean everything to me over the years, and his death while on a job in Whittlecombe in East Devon had been devastating. It had therefore been a real joy to be reunited with him. Having him at the agency, offering advice and doing research for me, even if it was in spirit form, was a proper boon for the Wonderland Detective Agency.

I'd only recently opened my new business. Having tried—and failed—to find alternative work to my responsibilities at the Ministry of Witches, I'd realised that actually, my first love was detecting. That's where my skills and my passion lay, and it made sense to carry on doing that—but as a private investigator rather than a public servant who had little choice in what cases to work on and who could be sent here, there and every-where on the whim of my bosses. I'd named my busi-ness Wonderland because of the coincidence between my name and that of Alice Liddell from the Lewis Carroll classic.

But also, because Hattie, my landlady, was obsessed with the books and the characters and because the Wonderland offices were situated in the attic above her mad hat shop.

"Oh, I don't know what to choose," I groaned. For the life of me, I couldn't decide who would prefer which cake or bun.

A tiny old woman standing next to me and casting an eye over the loaves peered up at me and grinned. "Have one of each, chicken. That's the best way."

"Like a selection, you mean?" That seemed to be a good idea. We could share them out.

"It won't do your figure much good, but you'll die happy." She chortled and carried on along Tudor Lane.

Wise words.

I made my way inside the shop, stooping to get through the entrance. The ceiling was so low, and the wooden floorboards beneath my feet so spongy, I could never quite shake the feeling that the weight of the old building was crushing the tiny shop below itself. I joined the queue at the counter. Eventually I was served by Julie, Betty's great-granddaughter. Betty had been dead for at least fifty years, bless her, but she still occupied a corner of the shop, pounding the living daylights out of bread dough, always kneading and spraying flour around. Oh yes. It was like a perpetual snowstorm behind the counter of Betty's Bakery.

"Please may I have an assortment of cakes," I said.

"I'll take eight." I waved my hand vaguely in the direction of the display in the window.

"Any eight?" Julie asked.

"Yes please," I nodded. Then, thinking about it, added, "but can you make sure there's a custard finger doughnut among them?"

Julie grinned. A custard finger doughnut was my regular order. She picked up her tongs and began to fill a cardboard tray with delicacies.

"You should try my custard slice," Betty said, without looking up from her dough. "It's the best in the business."

Julie glanced sideways at me, so I nodded. "Aye, go on." I watched as she picked up a rectangular brick dripping in white icing. "Wow!" I exclaimed. "I've never seen one that size before! We might have to save some of these till the morning. There's only four of us."

"Always best eaten on the day of purchase," Betty said.

Julie, closing the box, winked at me. "That way, you can come and buy some more tomorrow. It all keeps us in profit."

"That's as good a reason as any to buy a tray full of cakes," I agreed, and handed over a tenner and some change.

"Mind how you go," Julie called as I waved goodbye.

Back outside in Tudor Lane, I wobbled across the cobbles. Hanging between the buildings, the streetlights on their iron brackets had blinked on while I'd been inside. It was only half past three. The days were getting longer, but the cramped layout of Tumble Town—with its narrow paths and meandering alleys, its three-storey historic buildings, and the way the structures leaned in towards each other as though whispering secrets unfit for anyone on the ground to hear—effectively cut the daylight out relatively early.

Not that the inhabitants of Tumble Town minded. Oh no. Far from it! A simmering cauldron of vagabonds, ruffians and miscreants were crammed into this small town hidden behind Celestial Street, edging up to the banks of the River Thames. Every witch, wizard, warlock, gnome, soothsayer, fortune teller, medium, conjurer, sage, mage and quack—in fact, any paranormal being who had something to hide—found a welcome in Tumble Town.

I'd never imagined—being for all intents and purposes a 'good' law-abiding witch—that I would want to live here, but the truth was, that since taking on a small apartment on Bath Terrace overlooking Peachstone Market, I'd begun to feel strangely at home. The market, operating Wednesday to Sunday, was lively and full of colour. I could get everything I needed there at a reasonable price. I'd already begun to have a nodding acquaintance with some of the stall-holders who recognised me as I came and went. I suppose, with the rainbow streaks in my hair, I was hard to miss.

A couple of children ran towards me, shrieking in delight, one of them colliding with my knees. "Oi!" I shouted, visions of my cakes flying through the air, but they'd already disappeared down the lane, heading in the eventual direction of Cross Lane. A few seconds later I heard the popping of caps and a woman shrieking.

*Little boggers*, I thought to myself.

I steadied myself—and the all-important cakes—and carried on, hoping that Wootton had the kettle on.

Charles Lynch, the landlord of The Pig and Pepper—a pub I now considered my local—was standing on the front step, scowling at passers-by who had the audacity to stroll past but not pop in. He was a tall, rotund man in his late fifties, almost completely bald, with a pink whiskery face and the most depressing demeanour. He rarely had anything good to say about anyone and was permanently grumpy. Today he was wearing a blood-stained apron because he was head chef as well as proprietor, although I had never eaten within his dark establishment. I could only assume business was slow.

"Good afternoon, Charles," I smiled as I came level with him.

He curled his lip into a sneer and scratched his back-side. "What's good about it?"

I should have known better than to start a conversation with him. I'd end up feeling as gloomy as him if I hung around him for long. I made a conscious effort to retain a cheerful disposition. "It's Wootton's birthday today!" I told him and instantly could have kicked myself for mentioning it.

"The Wootton you stole from me, you mean?" I'd first met Wootton when he worked behind the bar of The Pig and Pepper. He'd proven to have good instincts and a curious mind and, knowing that he was good with computers and things of that ilk, I'd recruited him as soon as I set up my office. He hadn't taken much persuading to join me.

"Technically, I didn't steal him. He was already looking for other work," I pointed out.

"But he hadn't found any, had he?" Charles argued.

I had to concede that point. Deciding to change the subject, I held up my box of buns. "In honour of Wootton's birthday, I visited Betty's Bakery. Would you like one of my cakes, Charles?"

He snorted. "Not good for your figure, are they?"

What was *he* talking about? He must have been six feet tall and half as wide. He'd never watched his figure in his life. I pulled open the lid of the box so that he could see the wondrous selection. His beady eyes lit up immediately.

"That's an awful lot of loveliness, I must say. How many have you got there?"

The poor man obviously couldn't count. "Nine."

"I'm only surprised you have that many friends," he said. "Is that one of Betty's custard slices I spy there?" Before I could confirm it was, he dug his filthy stubby fingers into the assortment and pulled out the brick-sized cake that Betty had recommended to me. "Here you are love, you can keep that." He thrust the accompanying napkin back into the box.

"Cheers," I said.

"No problem." He swivelled away.

"I might see you later," I told him. "We'll pop in for a celebratory drink after work."

He looked back over his shoulder, a smear of icing

on the side of his mouth. "If you must. You're not good for business, though."

I raised my eyebrows. "*I'm* not good for business?" How much had I spent in there recently? I was subsidising the whole establishment.

"Everyone knows you're an ex-copper and that in truth, you're still working for them."

"I am not!" I protested.

He pointed the vanilla slice at me. "But you *are* still a detective."

"Yes." I could hardly deny that.

"There you are then." He took a huge bite of cake and chewed, crumbs scattering down his front. "You put my clientele off," he said with his mouth full.

*You shouldn't have such a dodgy clientele*, I wanted to say to him, but that would have been neither diplomatic nor fair. This was Tumble Town, not Celestial Street. His punters, by and large, were exactly who you'd expect them to be.

"If we do come in," I volunteered, "I'll keep a low profile."

He grunted and disappeared inside.

I scowled after him before I realised he'd managed to turn me into as big a sourpuss as he was. Sighing in exasperation, I carefully closed the lid on my precious cakes and continued on my way.

The lane became gloomier as I walked along. The top storeys of the buildings on either side leaned in, almost banishing the light. The cobbles in front of The Hat and Dashery sparkled a welcome as I approached, the gentle glow of the illuminated window display spilling warmly into Tudor Lane. It gave me a little thrill to see the building lit up that way. On the top floor, Wootton had turned the lights on in the office. I just needed to give Hattie a shout, then she and I could traipse upstairs and get our little tea party underway. She'd promised to lend me some of her finest cups and saucers—Hattie only ever drank out of bone china—so I needed to organise that too. At Hattie's instigation, I'd already invested in a large teapot for the office, and she'd knitted a bright tea cosy for me from scraps of wool she had left over from one of her decorated top hat projects. Like her, it was oddly and endearingly quirky.

I was almost there when a flash of white, low to the ground, caught my eye. It skirted the disused factory building opposite The Hat and Dashery before slipping into the shadows. I paused and cocked my head. My last encounter in that old factory had been a little alarming, so I wasn't in a hurry to venture inside.

What I'd seen had probably been a cat. There were thousands of them in Tumble Town, as you might imagine. They tended to be the favoured familiar of most witches, and plenty of wizards to boot, of course.

I approached the factory with caution, unwilling to go after the wretched thing if it decided to make a dash for the inside, but it didn't. The building had been properly fortified by some security company who had been called in by my ex-boss DCI Monkton Wyld after our little run-in a couple of months previously.

At that time, I'd been pursuing DC Cerys Pritchard, another of my ex-colleagues, who I believed to have murdered a wizard named Elryn Dodo, the previous occupant of the office I now inhabited. She had been working with a younger DC named Kevin Makepeace and a shadowy group that I had so far been unable to find out much about. The motive for Dodo's murder had been the theft of a 'key'—actually a magickal device disguised as a bog-standard notebook—that could identify and reveal powerful dark spells.

Wizard Dodo, a spellcaster and spell archivist, had used this notebook as a 'lock' to disguise and conceal these hexes. He had made it his mission to eliminate the blackest of evils that he came across as he sorted through grimoires, letters, books and journals dating back decades and even hundreds of years.

Makepeace had disappeared, but, thankfully, Cerys was languishing in Witchity Grubbs. Wyld and my old colleagues had made no progress so far in getting her to discuss the crime, let alone squeeze a confession from her. She would simply stare into space whenever anyone tried to talk to them. The evidence against her was fairly compelling, however. They had found the letter opener she had used to commit the murder wrapped in a scarf and hidden in the drawer of her desk at work. Forensic examination had proved that the letter opener was identical to the one Wizard Dodo had kept on his desk, but most persuasive of all, the blood on the blade was a match to his.

I expected to be called to give evidence at her trial at some stage, and I would be more than pleased to do so. Finding Wizard Dodo's murderer had felt personal, although it was a shame I hadn't been able to find the others who had been involved.

As I came level with the doorway of the disused factory, I realised that the thing I was following wasn't a cat after all, but a rabbit. The prettiest snowy white rabbit I had ever seen. Not that I'd seen many. I didn't spend much time in the countryside, to be fair. It wasn't really the kind of environment I thrived in. I preferred the grime and the noise and the sin of the city to the muck of the earth and the stench of farm animals. And besides, the city kept me in business when all was said and done.

How many murders occurred out in the sticks?

Not enough to keep my detective agency busy, I'd warrant.

"Hey," I said, wrinkling my nose at the little fellow. It sat back on its hind legs, its whiskers twitching, regarding me with a wary expression. It occurred to me that you don't find many white rabbits in the wild in the UK. Surely our native rabbits are a kind of beigy-browny-creamy-grey-ey type of colour? It also occurred to me that not many rabbits lived in Tumble Town full stop. Rats-a-plenty, yes, but not rabbits.

Which meant this one might be a pet. And if it was a pet, perhaps it had escaped from its pen in someone's back yard.

"Are you lost?" I asked, hoping it would reply. It didn't though. It just twizzled its whiskers. "Is someone looking for you?"

*Twitch, twitch, twitch.*

"Right." I glanced around, pondering on whether the

rabbit's sudden appearance had something to do with the kids who had been running amok down the lane a few moments before. Typically, there was no-one in sight that I could ask. I peered behind me. Hattie had come to the door of The Hat and Dashery and was squinting out at me.

I slowly walked backwards so as not to alarm the rabbit.

Hattie pulled the door open. "What are you doing, Elise?" she asked.

Handing over the box of cakes, I indicated the rabbit. "Look," I said. "Do you think he might belong to someone?"

Hattie scrutinised the shadows. I think she needed spectacles but was probably too vain to wear them. "What am I looking at?"

"There!" I hissed. The rabbit obligingly stepped forwards and presented itself.

"Oh, my witchy word! It's a white rabbit! How cute!" Hattie jiggled in excitement. Once again, I feared for the safety of my cakes. "Go and get it, Elise!"

"What would we do with a rabbit?" I wanted to know.

"We'll have to try and find its owner, I suppose." She widened her eyes. "And if we can't, we'll keep it! It's so pretty!"

The rabbit, perhaps aware that we were discussing it, hopped a little closer.

"You see?" Hattie sounded jubilant. "It wants to come and live with us. It looks perfectly tame. Pick it up, Elise."

"What?" I shrank away from it. "I don't know how to pick up a rabbit!"

"How hard can it be?" Hattie thrust the box of cakes back towards me. "Here. You grab these. I'll go and get it."

I stared down at the creature. It batted huge soft brown eyes at me. Dang! It was adorable. Nothing that sweet could hurt me, surely? "No, it's alright," I said, stepping towards it. "I'll grab him."

It took a few tentative hops up the lane, back in the direction it had come. I timidly followed it, hoping it would remain calm. "Here, bunny wunny," I said.

Every step I took, it made an equal number of hops away from me, as though we were playing a game. "You're a little rascal!" I gently chided it, still intent on coaxing it towards me. It wasn't playing by my rules, however. At the edge of the factory was a small ginnel, an entranceway to a narrow alley that ran between the tightly crammed buildings. The rabbit paused there, waiting for me to catch up, until, once I was within touching distance, it hopped away into the darkness.

"Oh, you're kidding me," I grumbled. I glanced behind me.

Hattie was watching my progress in amusement. "Go on!" she called, and giggled.

I huffed in annoyance but drew out my boringly ordinary police issue wand. "*Illuminate*," I told it, and the tip lit up, allowing me to see a little further along the narrow alley. The rabbit had disappeared.

Cursing my luck, I stole quietly along the litter-strewn path, manoeuvring carefully around piles of rubbish, sodden clothes, plastic bags, a couple of battered old bicycles and a bag of concrete that had set solid after being dumped here. Plaster fell from the wall to my right, exposing the old Victorian red brick of the factory's walls. To my left, a high wall hid the houses on that side from my view. Every now and again, I'd pass a gate, firmly locked against trespassers.

I followed the sound of my scampering long-eared friend. He trod quietly, but with so much detritus in the alleyway, it wasn't hard to track him whenever he disturbed something. The occasional flash of white helped too.

The alleyway came to an abrupt end ahead of me, the wall bricked up to prevent further progress, but at the same time I came to the far edge of the factory on my right. Between the brick wall and the rear of the factory was a double wooden gate, wide, as though to admit deliveries. Why it had to be that size when you'd have little chance of even leading a horse down the alley, I had no idea. The gate was old, probably not original, but if I'd had to guess, I would say it hadn't been replaced for about forty years or more. There was a gap in one corner where the rabbit might have slipped underneath. I pressed my hand against the gate, checking its solidity. It scraped along the floor when I gave it an exploratory push.

But it wasn't locked. There was no chain and no padlock. Not even a latch.

I found that odd.

I shoved the gate open, just wide enough to allow myself through the gap, and swung the illuminated tip of my wand about, casting light into the gloom. There was more rubbish in here, piles of it. A mattress. A couple of sleeping bags. Clothes. It looked as though several people had been living rough for a while and then discarded their belongings when they moved on. Glancing up, I could see the rear view of the factory. The tall, arched windows on the ground floor were now completely boarded up, along with the large sash windows on the first floor designed to let in plenty of light for the workers. There were likely shorter versions of those on the top floor.

I stared at the top floor a long way above me, remembering the terrifying incident with the mysterious robed figure just a couple of months ago. After attacking me, it had escaped by bursting through the glass on the Tudor Lane side, dropping from a great height and disappearing without a trace. And all without hurting itself.

If it was a long way up, it was a long way down too.

I shuddered.

A sudden clicking noise from the ground in front of me caught my attention and I glanced down. The rabbit had reappeared and was now rubbing its front paws together and making the peculiar sound. It was almost as though it was talking to me. When I shone my wand that way, it ducked its head. I dropped the beam, not wanting to blind the poor creature.

"Are you coming with me or not?" I asked it. "It's a bit spooky round here."

It held my gaze for a few seconds then hopped to the left.

I watched it go and rolled my eyes. "You know, I haven't got all day," I told it. "There are cakes to be eaten and tea to be drunk." I stepped after it. It skipped another few feet away, then stopped in front of the mattress.

"And it stinks around here." I wrinkled my nose and stepped towards the rabbit, this time with more determination. Either it let me pick it up, or I was going back to the office without it.

"I can't help you unless you help yourself," I told it.

Finally, it stayed in place. With a sense of jubilation, I leaned down to scoop it up.

And jerked backwards.

Something smelt really wrong.

Forgetting the rabbit, I lifted my wand and directed the light towards the mattress and the bundle of clothes and sleeping bag that were piled there.

Except … it wasn't a bundle of clothes.

It was a man.

And I didn't have to get any closer to see that he was very, very dead.

CHAPTER 2

"You can't keep away from this place, can you?" DCI Monkton Wyld had turned up to supervise his investigating team. When I'd called it in, I hadn't known who would attend the incident, my ex-colleagues from the Ministry of Witches Police Department's murder squad, or an equivalent representative from the Dark Squad.

The Dark Squad were the shadowy underbelly of the Ministry of Witches. Nobody, not even Monkton, knew much about them. It was rare for the two branches to co-operate. What this meant in practice was that you could toss a coin if there was a murder on this side of Celestial Street and just wait and see who would show up.

But given that I'd been the one to find the body, I'd fully expected it to be handled by my old team.

"Har-de-har," I said. "I'll have you know I have a party to go to."

"A party? It's a bit early in the day to be going to parties."

"A tea party. It's Wootton's birthday. I'd only been sent out to buy cakes. I was on my way back."

Wyld gazed around in evident distaste. His team were busy erecting some portable lights. They wouldn't want to wait until morning to get started. It was likely to rain, and that would wash away any evidence there might be. I didn't imagine there would be much of that. The body hadn't looked particularly fresh to me.

*Eww.*

"You were sent out to buy cakes? What were you doing round the back of this place?" Wyld asked. "It's a strange place to be hanging out."

"I wasn't hanging out," I retorted. "I'm not fourteen."

"Oh, that's right. I forget, what with you looking so young and organising *tea* parties and all." He smirked at me. "So you were sneaking around, then? I thought we'd laid all that Dodo business to rest."

"How have we laid it to rest?" I couldn't help the edge of indignance that crept into my voice. I knew he was trying to needle me. I don't think he'd quite forgiven me for decking him in The Pig and Pepper the night we went in pursuit of Cerys.

Or for leaving the MOWPD, come to that.

He still had an angry pink line across the top of his nose where it was healing. He rubbed at it, sensing my scrutiny, trying and succeeding in making me feel guilty.

"We have Cerys in custody," he said, closing down that avenue of conversation. That was it. As far as

Monkton was concerned, Cerys in custody was all we needed. Wizard Dodo's murder case was closed. "So, what were you doing here?"

"I followed a rabbit."

Monkton blinked in surprise, then laughed. "You followed a rabbit?" He leaned forward to sniff my breath.

"You know I'm off the booze," I reminded him. "I'm not crazy. I spotted a white rabbit out in Tudor Lane, and Hattie had me follow it."

"She fancied it for her supper?" Monkton grimaced. He was a vegetarian.

"She wanted to either find its owner or rehome it, I think." I shrugged. "It was a gorgeous-looking rabbit."

"Uh-huh." He gestured pointedly at my empty hands. "You didn't manage to catch it though?"

"No." I regretted that. "In all the furore of the immediate aftermath of finding the body, it skipped off."

"Hopped. I think you'll find rabbits hop, Liddell."

"Whatever. It skedaddled."

"Probably wise." He sighed. "I wish I could."

We stood together, watching everyone else work. "What do you reckon?" Monkton asked. "Someone sleeping rough?"

"It certainly looks that way, doesn't it?" A worn tarpaulin covered what had once been a stable or something similar in the corner of the yard. A third of the roof had collapsed, the walls were decaying. It stood to reason that someone had spent some time sheltering from the weather in there. "We found a couple of mattresses in the factory, do you remember?" I reminded him.

"That's right."

"Maybe they had been living inside the factory, but after you guys boarded everything up, he or she was forced to come and live in the yard."

Monkton puffed his cheeks out. "That's a rum do, that."

"Always."

"I'm hoping this is an open and shut case. A drug overdose. Or something easily explained."

"Not very nice for the relatives," I told him.

"But at least I'll be able to clock off before midnight."

"DCI Wyld?" The pathologist on call, a huge Irishman by the name of Mickey O'Mahoney, gestured Monkton over to where he was crouched next to the body, working diligently with his younger, slimmer and entirely more attractive colleague, Ruby Bilton. I followed closely behind. I shouldn't have really, but I did so out of habit, eager to hear what Mickey had to say.

"What have you got for me?" Monkton asked. I knew he had everything crossed that Mickey would make things easy for him.

"What I have is a deceased white male, roughly late twenties, I would say. He's been dead for a few days—"

"A few?" Wyld asked, his voice sharp. The police deal in certainties. They have to if they want to get their cases to court.

"I can give you a better idea once we have him back at the morgue."

Monkton grunted. "Any idea—"

"What killed him?" Mickey spoke over him. "Again, I have to wait until we get him back to the morgue, but I'm going to hazard a guess that it wasn't natural causes."

"Genius," Wyld muttered. I was tempted to nudge him in the ribs with my elbow but decided that wasn't really my place. I knew from long experience that if you cajoled and coaxed Mickey, you got far more out of him than if you simply barked questions his way. Even better, if you had all the time in the world, just letting him do his job and reflect on what he found often proved to be the most illuminating method of learning more about the victim.

He knew his stuff, did Mickey.

"Did you find any drug paraphernalia?" Monkton asked.

Mickey shook his head. "Not our job."

"I know that. I just wondered whether he had anything stuffed inside that sleeping bag he's in."

"He's not *inside* the sleeping bag." Mickey reached out with a gloved hand and lifted it up to demonstrate. Monkton and I stepped back in unison.

"Steady as you go." Monkton pressed the back of his hand to his nose.

"He was *covered* in the sleeping bag, but he wasn't inside it," Mickey said.

"If this was foul play, perhaps someone was trying to hide the body?" I suggested.

"It's not great camouflage, is it? Not really." Monkton sounded thoughtful rather than disdainful.

"The thing is, how many people ever come around here?" I asked. "I didn't even know the factory had a yard."

"I've found a wallet!" Ruby called in excitement. "Just here next to his thigh."

The crime scene photographer stepped in to get some contextual shots, then leaned even closer to get some close-ups. He shifted position and snapped a few more.

"Good?" Monkton had been waiting patiently for the photographer to get what he needed.

"Yes, sir," the photographer nodded.

"Excellent!" Monkton fumbled in his pockets for a pair of latex gloves and snapped them onto his hands in a well-practised motion. He gently took the wallet from Ruby and held it in the palm of his right hand. "Shine your wand this way, Elise."

I did as he asked. "Good quality leather," I volunteered. "A little worse for wear."

"Seen some use," Wyld agreed and flipped open one side. There wasn't much in it. A few credit cards. They'd all been stuffed into one compartment as though someone had rifled through them and found nothing of interest. "We should get a name off one of these," Wyld said.

Knowing who the victim was always gave us a head start on any case we were investigating.

He pulled one out and held it carefully by the edges. "Oh, no."

Something heavy in Wyld's voice chilled me to the bone. "What is it?"

"This." Wyld plucked another of the cards from among the bunch. I recognised it immediately for what it was.

So did everyone else.

The world became still.

A warrant card. A Ministry of Witches Police Department warrant card.

The surface was grimy. I couldn't make out the detail. I wanted to ask 'who' but couldn't find the voice.

Monkton wiped away the dirt.

Detective Constable Kevin Lloyd Makepeace.

We'd found Cerys's missing partner-in-crime.

# CHAPTER 3

I arrived back at the offices of the Wonderland Detective Agency just before six thirty. A detective agency with its own offices makes it sound grand, but it really isn't.

The office was housed in the attic room of The Hat and Dashery building. It had once been a small flat that Hattie had inhabited while her mother was alive. After Mrs Dashery's death, Hattie had moved into the more spacious apartment on the middle floor of the building, directly above the shop, and let the attic space to Wizard Dodo to use as an office.

I had spent a little money on freshening the place up: nice flooring, apricot paint on the walls, prints and plants—Wootton took care of these; there wasn't a lot of point in me doing so—and some new desks in the front office for Wootton and Ezra for when we needed to work as a team. But I'd also utilised the other small room as a private office and installed a new desk for my own use in there. It turned out, though, that I preferred working at Dodo's desk in the main office with everyone else. I enjoyed the buzz of everyone working together.

Perhaps I missed the giant communal office I'd once shared with all the other Serious Crime Officers at the MOWPD.

Besides, the tiny back office wasn't ideal. There was a small kitchenette in there, and the bathroom fed directly off it as well. Needs must, however, and it made a useful space to hold confidential conversations. Hattie had rented the whole attic to me at a minuscule rent, so I wasn't complaining.

Hattie, Snitch, Wootton and my ghost-bestie Ezra were waiting for me as I finally made it back, a full three hours after heading out to Betty's.

"Where have you been?" Hattie asked. "I thought you'd be five minutes!"

"We were considering calling the police," Wootton said, "but Ezra said not to bother."

Ezra, lounging back in his chair with his feet on the desk, inspected his fingernails.

"Thanks very much, Ezra," I said. "It's good to know you're looking out for my wellbeing. Anything might have happened to me."

He raised his eyebrows without looking up at me. "Things don't happen to you, Elise. You know it. They happen to everyone around you."

He had a point. I generally found myself in the middle of the unexpected. Chaos and catastrophe tended to unfold all around me.

"The police were out anyway," said Snitch. He was

sitting on a chair at the same desk as Hattie, cradling one of her delicate cups and saucers. Given his appearance—lank hair and worn, scruffy trench coat, trousers that were too big for him, slight features and scared, shifty eyes—the manner in which he held the cup, with his pinky outstretched, was a sight to behold.

"How did you know that?" Wootton asked. "I didn't see them!"

Snitch shrugged. "I just know."

Ezra snorted. "He can probably smell them, eh? Is that true, Snitch? Isn't it the case that you're usually either running away from them or spilling the beans to them about what your neighbours are up to—"

"Hey!" Snitch sounded hurt. "I was only ever an informant for you."

"Boys!" I interrupted. "Stop bickering. Is there any more tea in that pot?" I looked hopefully at Hattie.

"I'll make some fresh," she volunteered and, picking up the teapot, bustled out the back to put the kettle on.

I slid over to Dodo's desk where the box of cakes had been placed, but when I lifted the lid, all that greeted me was a layer of crumbs and a couple of smears of cream. "What the—"

"We were hungry," said Snitch.

"But—" I protested.

"And it is *my* birthday," Wootton nodded.

"And bored," Snitch added. "Boredom always makes me eat more."

"I don't believe you guys. There's only three of you!" Ezra, being a ghost, couldn't eat anyway. How had the others managed to put away eight cakes between them?

"Top drawer," Ezra said.

"Huh?" I eyed my ex-partner distrustfully. He was still maintaining his air of insouciance.

"Top drawer," he repeated slowly as though I were a simple creature who couldn't understand English.

I pulled the top drawer of Dodo's desk open and there, arranged neatly on a plate with a lace doily and a folded napkin, was my custard finger. *Huzzah!* "Thank you!"

I sank gratefully into my chair, glad to be taking the weight off my feet, and groaned.

"So, what have you been up to?" Ezra asked, and I heard the simmering curiosity in his voice. He, like me, loved the scent of trouble. It's what we'd built our careers on.

"I have good news and bad news," I told him.

"Okay. Sounds interesting." He sat up.

Hattie picked that moment to return with the teapot. "Just let it brew a while," she said and set it beside me along with a cup and saucer and a little jug of milk.

I nodded my thanks and dipped my finger into the custard of my cake, then licked it clean. *Mmm.* Heavy on the vanilla and a nice thick consistency.

"Tell us!" Wootton slapped his hands on his desk.

Jabbing my damp finger onto the sugary surface of the doughnut, I wobbled my head. "The good news is that I located DC Kevin Makepeace."

"Who is Kevin Makepeace again?" Hattie asked. She could be a little slow on the uptake at times.

"Cerys Pritchard's partner. He went missing after Wizard Dodo's murder," Wootton reminded her. I'd made him type up all my case notes relating to the crime, so he was intimately familiar with what had gone on.

"Oh, that's right," Hattie nodded, although the blank look in her eyes suggested she still wasn't following.

"You found him?" Ezra prompted me.

"I almost stumbled over him while chasing the rabbit."

Hattie sat up straight, and I could see the next question in her eyes.

"The bad news is that I didn't find the rabbit," I told her. She looked hurt, as though my inability to bring the rabbit home was a personal affront to her. "It ran off!" I felt the need to defend my lack of rabbit hunting and trapping skills.

"And—" Ezra knew there was more.

I stared pointedly back at him. "DC Makepeace was dead."

"Ah." He resumed studying his fingernails.

"I don't understand," Hattie said, and I thought she was going to ask me how I'd let the rabbit escape. But she didn't. "If he was involved in Wizard Dodo's murder, isn't it a good thing that he's dead?"

"That's harsh, Hattie." Even Wootton looked taken aback.

I understood her feelings on the matter, although I didn't generally believe in an eye for an eye. "The thing is, it would have been good to find him and see if he would talk to us about his involvement. We still don't know how it all fits together or who Cerys was working with."

She nodded. "Fair do's, I suppose."

From below, we heard the clunk of the front door opening and heavy shoes on the bottom flight of stairs.

"Helloooo?" a familiar voice.

"Monkton," I said.

"Is Makepeace his case?" Ezra asked.

"Yep. I called it in and he attended."

"I suppose we'd better make ourselves scarce." Hattie stood and began collecting cups and saucers. Snitch, who'd lodged himself next to the door ready to make a run for it as soon as Monkton walked into the office, was already buttoning up his shabby trench coat.

"You don't have to," I told them.

Wootton closed down his computer. "We'll meet you in the pub," he said. "I'll get you a sparkling water."

"Great, thanks!" *Not*. Being on the wagon was grim, at times.

Monkton climbed onto the landing and met my eye. "Sorry," he said. "I didn't realise you had company."

"They're not company," I told him. "They're my team." I beckoned him in. As soon as he stepped inside, Snitch darted out of the door. He'd run down the stairs in less time than it took for Monkton to nod hello at everyone else.

"You're all leaving?" he asked.

"My birthday," Wootton smiled as he walked past him, ushering Hattie ahead of himself. "We're going to celebrate at The Pig and Pepper. You're welcome to join us."

"Sounds good," Monkton replied, but without much enthusiasm.

"See you in a bit," I yelled as they disappeared. Only Ezra had stayed behind.

"Is that tea in that pot?" Monkton asked. In the better illumination of the office, I could see the dark circles framing his eyes that hadn't been so visible when we'd spoken in the yard.

"It is. Fresh too!" I stood. "Let me grab you a mug." By the time I'd returned from the kitchenette in the back office, he had made himself comfortable at Wootton's desk and was playing with a Newton's Cradle desk toy.

I poured tea for both of us. He preferred his black but spooned half a dozen teaspoons of sugar into the mug. *Ugh.*

"So, what's up?" I asked. "What brings you here?"

"Oh, you know, the small matter of you finding a body less than a hundred yards from where you're currently sitting drinking tea and eating a cake."

I blinked. "*I* didn't kill Makepeace." What was Monkton insinuating?

"Of course you didn't," Monkton growled and rubbed his eyes. "But what does it look like?" He pointed at my cake. "Are you going to eat that?"

"That was the plan." I was relieved Monkton didn't seriously think I'd had anything to do with the death of the DC.

"Top drawer," said Ezra.

"What?" Monkton asked.

"Top drawer," Ezra repeated. Monkton pulled open the top drawer of Wootton's desk and withdrew a cream horn, coated in sugar and drizzled with caramel,

THE RABBIT HOLE MURDERS

arranged as mine had been, on a doily on a plate. "Phwoar!" Monkton didn't think twice; he scooped it up and bit off a huge chunk. Cream squirted over Wootton's pristine desk.

"I really hope Wootton wasn't saving that for tomorrow," I said.

"Gotta keep the boss happy," Ezra said, nodding at Monkton.

"I'm your boss," I reminded him. "He's your old boss."

Ezra only shrugged.

"So, was there something you needed from me?" I pressed Monkton.

He wiped his fingers on a paper napkin and took a swig of tea. "They're leaving the body in situ overnight so they can get a better look at the scene in the daylight."

"Makes sense." It was sad to think of the young DC lying there in such a way, however. I wondered if he had family somewhere. At least he wouldn't be alone tonight. Several of his ex-colleagues would be pulling an all-nighter, no doubt.

"I'm going to have the factory re-opened," he said. "I want to know if Makepeace had been living in there."

"Do you seriously think he'd been living rough since Wizard Dodo's murder?" I asked. I found that difficult to believe. "Right here on the doorstep?"

"Stranger things have happened," Monkton said, but he looked troubled.

Ezra caught my eye. "What are you thinking?" I asked Monkton.

He sighed. "I want to write this off as a coincidence."

"But you can't." It seemed obvious to me.

"No. No way. Pritchard and Makepeace were partners, then Dodo is killed, and we finger Pritchard for it while Makepeace does a runner."

"You never actively pursued that avenue," I reminded him. I'd tried to persuade him that it would be a good idea to go after Makepeace, but for some reason he'd never thrown much weight behind it, assuming Makepeace was a missing person and not a person of interest.

"We had Cerys bang to rights," Monkton defended himself. "The most we'd have on Makepeace was that he'd be an accessory."

"An accessory to murder, though! Still worth following up in my book." I folded my arms and glared at my old DCI.

"It's all academic now, Elise. We've found him," Ezra pointed out.

"But dead men don't tell tales." I took a glug of my own unsweetened tea.

"Some do," Ezra grinned.

Monkton, ignoring him, frowned. "You were right, Elise. I should have put more time and energy into finding Makepeace."

I raised my eyebrows. Was Monkton actually conceding that I'd known best? Wonders would never cease. It was a hollow victory, however.

"The more I think about it," Monkton was saying, "the more troubled I am by what happened." He hesitated and leaned over his desk, looking first at me and then at Ezra. "Can I let you in on something?" he asked, his voice low.

"Of course," I said, and Ezra nodded.

"You're not to breathe a word of this." Monkton exhaled heavily. We waited for him to continue. Eventually, he said, "The night we brought in Pritchard and found the letter opener in her desk, I presented what we knew and what had happened to us in the disused factory to my manager."

"Superintendent Ibeus?" I asked. Yvonne Ibeus. A rather formidable woman, I had liked to stay out her way as far as possible.

"Yes." Monkton twiddled with the Newton's Cradle again, gathering his thoughts.

"I wanted to know if we should pursue those … people … those robed gangsters who attacked us, you remember?"

Why would I have forgotten? "Yes. The creatures Cerys was involved with."

"The super told me not to worry about it. She would send it up the chain of command and the Dark Squad would be alerted."

As frustrating as that was, it made perfect sense. Tumble Town was not generally our area of jurisdiction.

Ezra harrumphed. "Let me guess. Nothing happened."

"I assumed it had," Monkton said. "But I've just placed a call to Ibeus and you're right. She tells me nothing was actioned last time."

"But she's going to action it now, isn't she?" I asked. Surely her lack of action was a simple oversight?

"She sounded vague and non-committal," Monkton frowned. "Meaning we're no nearer to knowing what Pritchard and Makepeace were involved in."

"And now Makepeace can't tell us," I said, my insides twisting in irritation.

"Exactly." Monkton levelled his gaze my way. "*No-one* is looking into this mess. The question is, do we want to just let it go or do we pursue it?"

I waited, unsure what he was asking. What would Ibeus say if Monkton started poking his nose back in?

"What about Pritchard?" Ezra asked. "How would she react if she knew Makepeace was dead? How close was their relationship?"

This was a good point. Police partners often form strong bonds—as I knew from my devastating experience of losing Ezra. It was good to have him by my side again, even if he was a ghost.

"She's non-communicative." Monkton shook his head. "I've tried to interview her half a dozen times. She stares straight ahead, doesn't meet my eyes, has nothing to say. Her lawyer tells us they're trying to have her committed to a secure psychiatric unit."

"Hmpf. Copping the old insanity plea, is she?" I wouldn't generally be dismissive of anyone's mental health issues, but I couldn't help feeling cynical where Cerys was concerned. She and I had been good friends once upon a time, but after what she'd done, any sympathy I had for her had dissipated like steam out of an open bathroom window.

"Perhaps you should try?" Ezra was looking at me.

I wrinkled my nose. "What do you mean? Interview Cerys?"

"Yeah. You were buddies once."

"I can't interview her," I reminded him, "I'm a civilian now."

"But you can *visit* her," Monkton said. He'd perked up at the idea. "I could arrange something, I'm sure."

I thought about it for a moment. "It might be useful," I grudgingly admitted. "Will you let me break the news to her about Makepeace?"

"Oof," groaned Ezra, "you're cruel, Elise."

"Come on." I waved my finger at him. "I learned from the best. You were the one who taught me all the various ways of manipulating someone's emotions, how best to wrangle information from a reluctant witness."

"She's definitely one of the most reluctant witnesses I've ever come across," Monkton confirmed. "So you'll go?"

"I will," I agreed. "As soon as you can set it up."

CHAPTER 4

I was shown through to a meeting room in the women's hospital wing at Witchwood Scrubbs. The women's wing was slightly less grim than the men's wing, in that the air was fragranced by cheap deodorant and market-stall perfume as opposed to baked beans and stale farts, and the paint seemed fresher and the furniture slightly less chipped.

But there the positives ended.

The establishment had been fabricated from the same Victorian red brick as much of Tumble Town, and the architect had taken great delight in the idea that this was a 'house of correction', not a palace of pleasure. The windows were tall and narrow, arched at the top and protected by iron bars. The lighting was modern and bright, highlighting every depressing blemish and every flaw on every face, none of which had seen the sun in months.

The female prison officer, her badge informing me her name was Officer Caroline Shaw, showed me into a meeting room which, in and of itself, wasn't that bad. A large, old-fashioned television had been mounted on a heavy bracket, but other than that—and a whiteboard covered in obscene images that had been painted on in permanent marker rather than wipeable ink pens—there was nothing interesting to look at.

"Can I offer you a tea or a coffee, ma'am?" Officer Shaw asked.

"Coffee would be lovely," I said.

"It only comes in plastic cups, I'm afraid."

"That's fine." I didn't bother to tell her I knew all about the safety precautions in place from the many other visits I'd made in pursuit of witness statements. Why would she be interested? As far as she was aware, I was a civilian. I took a seat at the table, large enough for eight to ten people to gather round, and popped my notebook in front of me along with the pencil I'd been allowed to bring inside. Everything else, including my wand and mobile phone, had been locked away at the gate and I'd have to retrieve them on my way out.

She wasn't away long. I assumed there was a little office down the hall where she and the other officers hung out. "If you need anything else, give me a shout," she smiled as she deposited my drink.

"You won't be locking the door?" I asked. That surprised me.

"No. For the most part, the patients on this wing are so far gone, a sleepy toddler would be able to take them down if they started playing up."

"There's no trouble, ever?"

She laughed at my wide eyes. "Oh, there's plenty. Just

not on this floor. Don't worry, our most violent patients aren't allowed out of their rooms by and large."

*Interesting.* "Cerys Pritchard isn't considered dangerous?" I asked.

Officer Shaw shook her head. "No. From the moment she arrived—a transfer from the hospital, wasn't it?—she hasn't said a word."

"Do you think she's putting it on?" I decided to be blunt.

She shook her head. "If she is, she's a good actress. I don't know all the details of her case, but it's my understanding that the folk in the know think she's genuinely traumatised."

I filed that information away, pondering on how difficult it would be to talk to those 'folk in the know' about Cerys. Impossible, probably.

I wasn't doubting for one second that the psychiatric experts—both here at Witchity Grubbs and also at the hospital where she'd first been treated—knew what they were doing. However, it's worth bearing in mind that, in my long experience of attending court cases as a witness for the prosecution, the defence never failed to find an expert from somewhere who would swear the complete opposite of what the prosecution was alleging.

It could be frustrating at times.

A jangle of keys and a clang at the end of the hall signified that someone was coming. Officer Shaw popped her head out into the corridor, although there was no need. The entire fourth wall was made of glass. "Here she is," she said.

Another prison officer was escorting Cerys along

the hall. I stared aghast through the glass at the shadow of a woman I had known for a good six years or so—someone I had often been out drinking with on the nights when we both needed to unwind and commiserate about cases that were going nowhere, or celebrating when we'd got our man or woman bang to rights.

The escort ushered Cerys through into the meeting room. She did as she was told, although without any sign that she was processing the orders given to her, let alone questioning them. She trod lightly, as though she were of little substance, and only sat in the chair opposite when the guard told her to do so.

Officer Shaw nodded. "As I said, just holler if you need anything, or"—she pointed at a bright green button on the wall—"if you're in serious difficulty, slam that and it'll set the alarm off."

"No problem, thank you," I said, and waited for the officers to leave.

I settled back in my chair and scrutinised Cerys. Originally from the Welsh valleys, she'd always been a small and slim young woman, but now she had faded into herself. She seemed impossibly tiny. Her hair, once a thick shining black bob that I had secretly envied, was now patchy and thin as though someone had been pulling her hair out. Maybe she'd been doing it herself?

Her dark eyes were sunken, black circles pooled beneath them. Her skin, once porcelain, had become grey and dry.

My stomach churned. I hated to see her this way. What had happened to her? Who had she become involved with? Why had she agreed to do their bidding? None of it made any sense to me. I'd thought her a woman dedicated to her detective work.

How could I have read her so wrong?

I'd formulated a list of questions to ask, but now, my mouth dry, they went out of the window. I simply observed her, mutely searching for the answers that her tired, careworn exterior wouldn't give up.

While I watched her, time slipped away. With a jolt, I realised we'd been sitting silently for over five minutes.

In all that time, her eyes hadn't flickered. She had no facial tic. She hardly appeared to be breathing. She simply stared straight ahead, concentrating on a void that only she could see.

At last, I cleared my throat. "Cerys?" I asked.

No movement. No indication at all that she had heard me.

I continued regardless. I'd heard that people in a 'locked in' state could hear, even if they didn't respond. Weren't there cases of patients coming out of comas and being able to relay what had been said to them, when all outward signs would indicate they could not be reached?

"I know people have visited you before and that they wanted to ask you questions about your involvement in Wizard Dodo's murder …"

I paused, patiently examining her.

Nothing.

"The thing is, whereas some of my—our—ex-colleagues might think it's an open and shut case because they found the perpetrator, and that's the end of the matter, for me it isn't."

I toyed with my coffee, never taking my eyes from Cerys. "For some reason—perhaps because I was on the scene so early, perhaps because I have come to know a few of the people who loved him—I never stop thinking about him and the way he died."

Laughter drifted down the corridor. The prison officers were having a joke together.

"It's important to me to find out all the circumstances of what happened and why. Unlike some of our ex-colleagues, I fully intend to get to the bottom of it. I want to find out who you were working with."

I stopped and thought for a second. "Or perhaps not *with* but *for*?"

Still no change in expression. The woman had hardly blinked.

"Nobody else seems to be interested. I find that strange. It's almost like there's a cover-up of some kind." I laughed gently, as though the idea tickled me. "I mean, it wouldn't be the first time such a thing had happened. We all know the Ministry of Witches Police Department has had a long and chequered history when it comes to bent coppers. It's not easy being a witch and ratting on your mates. It's not easy to obey the rules when all around us, our friends and loved ones break the law because *that's* what so many witches and wizards do."

I sniffed and pretended to consider what I was saying. "But perhaps that isn't what happened here. If only I could find DC Makepeace." I stared Cerys straight in the eye. "Kevin, wasn't it? I didn't get to know him very well before I left, but I recall that he seemed a sweet young man. A diligent worker."

Opening my notepad, I flipped through several pages until I found what I was looking for. "He's what? Twenty-four? No, twenty-five, nearly twenty-six. He'd been working in uniform for about four years when he had the opportunity to transfer to us. He was no bright star, not as ambitious as you, but he was steady and that impressed DCI Wyld enough to hire him."

I tapped on my notebook with my pencil. "You were partnered up with him fourteen months ago after DC Farley went off on maternity leave. By all accounts, from what I can surmise—because some of our ex-colleagues are being very tight-lipped about you—you and DC Makepeace were getting on well."

I smiled. "*Very* well. In fact, so well, I'm wondering whether you were in a relationship?" I waited, as though I expected an answer.

None was forthcoming.

"No?" I queried. "Hmm. Okay. I might have the wrong end of the stick about that. The fact remains that he must have known what you did on the night you killed Wizard Dodo, because the police logs clearly show you were in Tumble Town together, and we have a witness who overheard police radios. That's *radios*. Plural. It incriminates the pair of you."

I shrugged as though that were no biggie. In actual fact it wasn't. Firstly, my witness was Snitch. This was unfortunate as, given his own lengthy record of minor misdemeanours, he wouldn't be a great witness for the

THE RABBIT HOLE MURDERS

prosecution. And in any case, a pair of twittering police radios was entirely circumstantial and unlikely to hold up in court.

But it was worth a bluff.

"I'm also interested in the person you met with at The Nautical Mile. Investigations are ongoing there."

That much was true. It was also fair to say I'd drawn a complete blank. If anybody knew anything about these odd creatures Cerys had been involved with, they weren't telling me.

And that included Snitch.

I took a swig of my rapidly cooling coffee. "My throat is getting dry. It's turning into a bit of a one-way conversation, this. Isn't it, Cerys? Wouldn't you like to contribute? There was a time when we never shut up. Do you remember?" I smiled. "What about that time we did the cancan on the table at Wyld's thirty-fifth birthday in The Full Moon? They almost threw us out for that. Wow. We were completely sozzled that night." It had taken me three days to recover from the resulting hangover. Grim.

"Good times," I enthused. "But now I find that the cat's got your tongue."

I leaned forward, not touching her, but close enough that I could smell her stale breath. "I really need to talk to someone about what happened. About who those people were. I want answers, Cerys. I'm sure you understand that."

I waited. Not a flicker of an eyelash.

She was hardcore.

I played my final hand.

Pushing my chair back, I rose. "Well, if you won't talk to me, I suppose I'll have to find someone who will. Perhaps I'll have better luck with DC Makepeace." I picked up my pencil and notebook, stood back and stared at Cerys with cold eyes.

"Except I won't. I can't do that now, can I? Three days ago, I found him. He was in the back yard of the disused factory opposite The Hat and Dashery." I paused. "Unfortunately, he was dead, Cerys. As dead as Dodo."

I waited, praying for a reaction. None came.

"Did the person who ordered you to kill Wizard Dodo come after Kevin too?"

She maintained her silence. I shrugged and walked to the door. "Alright. I'll leave that with you. No doubt we'll meet again in court." I turned the handle and stepped over the threshold into the corridor beyond. The smell of imitation Chanel No. 5 tickled my nose, threatening to make me sneeze.

I wanted her to jump up and tell me what she knew. But she didn't even twitch.

I gave her a few more moments and then, when she made no indication of having heard me at all, left her there. I strolled down the corridor and nodded at the prison officers.

"All done?" Officer Shaw asked. "Did she talk to you?"

"No, not a word," I said.

The other prison officer offered a wry shrug. "Yeah, she's not even remotely communicative. I'd best return her to her ward." She disappeared back the way I'd come.

"I'll show you out." Officer Shaw jangled her chain of keys and led the way to the nearest exit. I followed her through half a dozen gates, each of which needed to be unlocked and then re-locked. It was a lengthy process.

We were almost at the security reception when an alarm went off somewhere behind us. The radio the officer was carrying on her belt exploded into life. The clumping of dozens of pairs of heavy boots rang out in all directions, and from nowhere, prison officers exploded into view. Officer Shaw yanked me out of the way as the officers sprinted past me, then she thrust me through the final gate and locked it after me.

"You can make your way from here, can't you?"

"Yes, thank you," I replied, and with that, she turned tail and chased after her colleagues.

Although curious to know what was going on, it wasn't my place to find out, so I walked the last few yards to the reception area and waited for the gate officer to deal with me. It took a little while, given the furore somewhere in the prison, for the relevant paperwork to be prepared. I signed and went through the first set of glass doors. A second officer scrutinised my face, making sure I wasn't a convict who had cleverly managed to bribe my way this far, no doubt.

But at that moment, Officer Shaw came charging back. She banged on the glass door and breathlessly indicated that I should step back to her side.

I glanced at the officer in the security hub behind

the glass. He rolled his eyes, but the door slid open once more.

"What did you say to her?" Shaw was red-cheeked and wild-haired from running.

"What do you mean?" I asked.

"Pritchard's gone crazy. Took Officer Dowrie out with a single punch. In fact, it took eight officers to restrain her."

"Seriously?"

"They've managed to take her back to her cell now, and I expect she'll be sedated. But what did you say that upset her so much?"

I wriggled, uncomfortable under her scrutiny. "I broke the news that her ex-colleague had died," I told her. "She didn't show any sign of hearing me, let alone understanding me."

Shaw raised her eyebrows. "She obviously did."

"Indeed." I rolled my head back on my shoulders, thinking quickly. If Cerys had kicked off that badly then I must have been on to something. Perhaps she and Kevin had been more than colleagues.

Or perhaps she was scared that the wrath of the people she had been in league with had come another step closer to her door.

# CHAPTER 5

It was a gloomy afternoon. On my way back to the office, I grabbed a mocha from the Moonbucks in Celestial Street and sheltered from the rain beneath their canopy while I drank it. Typically, when I'd left Wonderland just before lunch, the skies had been blue and the weather pleasant. Now, in the space of just a few hours, you would be forgiven for imagining that it was going to rain forever.

And I had, of course, left my brolly by my desk.

One-handed, I plucked my phone from the pocket of my leather jacket and thumbed the screen to place a call to Monkton. It went to voicemail.

"Hey," I said. "Only me. Call me when you get this, and I can give you some interesting feedback about this afternoon." As I ended the call, a text came in from Wootton.

*Please pick up milk on your way back, Grandma.* He'd signed it W followed by a big X. I'd give him Grandma. And I'd carve a big X on his backside, the cheeky tyke.

I was about to send a suitable riposte when a flash of white in the corner of my eye caught my attention. I looked up.

"Are you pulling my leg?" I asked aloud.

Across the road from me, just at the intersection of Cross Lane, the main 'thoroughfare'—as in cramped little alleyway—into Tumble Town from Celestial Street, a rabbit crouched in the centre of the cobbles, carefully washing behind its ears.

A white rabbit. With bonny brown eyes.

Cute as you like.

*It can't possibly be the same one!*

I cast a wary glance around. Nobody else had noticed it. Or if they had, they were entirely unconcerned. People walked by it within kicking distance, in fact one or two came close to tripping over it or trampling it to death. I winced.

In the interests of wildlife preservation, I abandoned my dry spot under the Moonbucks' canopy and darted across the road. It stopped washing its ears and looked up at me with interest. "Hi," I said. "Remember me?"

It didn't seem afraid. I decided it probably wouldn't hurt me, unless it had fleas or was a bubonic plague-carrying bunny, at any rate. If I told Hattie I'd seen it again but still hadn't managed to catch it, she would not be best pleased. Tentatively, I reached down to pet it and realised that I wouldn't be able to pick it up unless I disposed of my coffee. In the few seconds it took me to stuff my phone in my pocket and locate the nearest rubbish bin, the rabbit had lost interest in waiting for me and disappeared.

"Great," I muttered. That had been a perfectly decent coffee, and only half drunk!

Sulking, my hair already wet from the rain, I decided I might as well brave the weather and get back to the office. I slipped into Cross Lane and, with my head tucked low against the drips from the buildings on either side of me—some of them didn't have any guttering whatsoever—I scurried on, reminding myself to buy milk somewhere along the way.

So preoccupied with my thoughts was I that I nearly missed the re-emergence of the rabbit until it was right under my feet. In trying to avoid it, I turned my ankle on the cobbles.

"Ow!" I supported my weight against the wall of the nearest building and glared at Mr Cutesy-Floppy-Ears. "Do you have a death wish or something?" I grumbled.

In answer to my question, the rabbit made a clicking noise and lolloped on ahead of me.

"I'm not following you," I told it.

Someone nearby snickered. "That's what you thinks." I stared into the doorway closest to me. Nothing there. Tumble Town could be weird at times.

The rabbit had paused when I'd spoken, but now it hopped away again. Realising I had no alternative, given that I didn't need to turn left for a while—I had to follow it for at least part of the way—I started after it. It happily gambolled along in front of me without a care in the world.

People coming towards me deigned not to see my furry companion, just as they avoided my eye, but I always had the sense that most Tumble Town residents observed everything.

I finally reached my turning. Fifty yards up this way and I would take a right and bear left and find myself in Tudor Lane. The rabbit pulled up at this point and turned back, staring at me again. It was almost as though it was double-daring me or something.

"I can take you back to the office with me," I suggested. "Nice cup of tea?"

It evidently didn't fancy a cuppa because it continued down Cross Lane for a few yards before turning to watch me once more.

I hesitated. It was raining. I was soaked. I wanted to get back to the office, where I had numerous cases awaiting my attention. But I hated to think of this pretty creature ending up in someone's pie, or some dark witch cutting off its paws to use as lucky rabbits' feet keyrings. That certainly wouldn't be lucky for the rabbit.

"Oh, dang and blast," I groused, and edged towards it.

Cleverly, it kept just out of my reach. I had a feeling that if I suddenly sprinted, it would accelerate away and leave me in its dust, so I kept my pace steady, hoping that at some stage I would be able to corner it.

Before that could happen, it took an abrupt right off Cross Lane. I glanced up at the street sign above my head. Packhorse Close.

A close! A road that didn't go anywhere! Perfect! The rabbit would have nowhere to go at the end of this!

I limped along behind it, convinced the end of the bunny saga was in sight. Packhorse Close was a tight space, with dozens of terraced houses, all crooked and run-down. The subdued glow of light from the front rooms that faced into the street was the only illumination down here. The space was so narrow there would have been no room for a bracket for a streetlight. Occasionally I lurched too close to the buildings and my shoulder grazed the brickwork.

Peering ahead, I realised I must be approaching the end of Packhorse Close. The final houses faded into shadow, more run-down than any I had passed so far. The passage had widened into an open space, the house on the left having been pulled down. The rabbit had stopped. It stood in the centre of the open space, in front of a brightly graffitied wall, staring at me, rubbing its little paws together, either in glee or anxiety. It was hard to tell.

"Ha!" I exclaimed. "Now I've got you! C'mere, bunny bunny bunny."

It remained in place and I walked right up to it and crouched in front of it, reaching out gently to pick it up, unsure how to hold it but assuming you could handle it by the scruff of the neck as you did cats.

Except as I bent forward, I caught a whiff of something ripe and meaty. Something entirely unexpected.

I gagged and twisted to my left. Nothing on the waste ground.

I retraced my steps, back past several of the disused houses.

There!

In a doorway, tucked well into the shadows so that I had missed it at first, was a humped shape. I edged closer, holding my breath so I wouldn't inhale any more of that awful stench. How had I missed it as I walked past?

Reaching out, I tentatively poked at the hump and rapidly drew my hand away. Pulling out my wand, I illuminated the scene, cursing at what I'd found.

*Another* body?

It lay twisted on its side, covered in a filthy khaki-coloured sleeping bag. With the edge of my wand, I probed gently. The sleeping bag covered the body; the body was not inside it.

In my pocket, my phone had begun to vibrate. I yanked it out. Monkton!

"Hi," he said. "Just returning your call. How did—"

I cut him off. "I'm in Packhorse Close. You have to get down here."

"What's going on?"

"Another body," I told him. "Bring lights. In fact, bring your whole team."

I heard him call out 'guys!' I could imagine him holding his hand up and demanding the attention of the whole squad back in our base room at the Ministry of Witches. Then he returned to our phone conversation. "Where exactly is Packhorse Close?"

"Tumble Town. Head towards the river. Keep an eye out for a right turn off Cross Lane."

He relayed that and I heard the bustle of people

THE RABBIT HOLE MURDERS

behind him. "What were you doing down there?" he asked.

"On another wild rabbit chase," I told him, swivelling around to locate my cute friend.

Funnily enough, he'd disappeared.

To be honest, I didn't blame him.

CHAPTER 6

"What are you thinking?" I shivered behind the tape on the edge of the crime scene. I'd been waiting for Monkton to come back to me, and he'd been taking his sweet time looking around and examining the scene. Dusk had fallen, along with the temperature. I hadn't dried off properly after the last rain shower, so was feeling rather chilly.

"It's another down and out," Monkton shrugged. "No immediate signs of foul play but a bit difficult to tell. We'll know more once Mickey gets him back to the morgue."

I studied Mickey's back. He was busy prodding the body or whatever pathologists do to try and ascertain cause and manner of death.

"Definitely someone sleeping rough, do you think?" I asked.

Monkton grimaced. "I reckon. His clothes, hair and hands are filthy. His skin is grimy, like he's been living in a coal mine."

"Old? Young?" I hadn't wanted to get too close to find out for myself.

"Relatively young. Early thirties maybe." He held his hand up. "And before you ask, no ID so far."

"Not another lost copper then?" I half-joked.

"That's not funny," Monkton said, but his eyes glittered. Gallows humour. Detectives love it.

I folded my arms across my chest and willed my teeth to stop chattering. "A bit of a coincidence though, isn't it?"

"What? This and Makepeace, you mean?"

I nodded. That was exactly what I meant.

Monkton wouldn't have it though. "Just how many people sleeping rough do you think turn up dead every year in London?" he asked.

"I honestly don't know," I answered.

"In 2018, there were nearly one hundred and fifty in London alone. That's one every few days. It's much more common than you might think."

"Homicides?" I asked.

"Mostly drug related or alcohol dependency. Quite a few suicides."

"That's so sad."

I stared back at the doorway where Mickey and Ruby were beavering away as the crime scene photographer tried to angle his camera over their shoulders.

"Do you have a cause of death for Makepeace yet?" I asked.

Monkton shook his head. "Preliminary findings were inconclusive. Mickey is going to have another crack at it."

"It looks like he'll be busy," I said, nodding in his direction.

"Long into the night, probably."

"Hmmm." I didn't want to tread on Monkton's toes, but I'd really like to get a sneaky peek at the findings of Makepeace's post-mortem. The problem with being a private investigator was that I had no grounds to gain access to such information.

There was a commotion behind us as two paramedics manhandled a gurney down the narrow alleyway. There was barely enough room for everybody who needed to be on hand as it was.

"It's a bit late for them, isn't it?" I snorted. "Tell you what. I'm going to make like a white rabbit and hop off. You'll find me in Wonderland if you need me."

Monkton grunted.

I saluted and turned to push my way through the thin crowd of spectators gathering on the other side of the police tape, agog at all the activity. Who could blame them? I felt equally curious.

Two bodies found in similar circumstances. Coincidence?

Maybe.

I wanted to know more.

I remembered to buy milk on my way to the office, but given that they had been expecting me several hours before, it was no surprise that Wootton had packed up for the day and gone home. Hattie was working late in her shop and Snitch was otherwise engaged—which, knowing Snitch, probably meant he was up to no good.

Only Ezra remained in the office, feet up on the desk, head on his chest, a trilby pulled down over his eyes.

"Are you asleep?" I asked, peeling off my outer layers of clothes and considering what to do about my jeans. Fortunately, my lightweight sweater was dry enough.

"Yes," he mumbled.

"You can't be tired. You haven't done anything all day," I pointed out. "You were in that exact same position when I left."

"My eyes are tired," he told me, "from staring at the screen all day."

I cast a dubious look at his computer. The screen was black.

"I take it you've been knee-deep in another homicide," he said. He hadn't even looked up at me yet.

"How did you know?" I decided, since he wasn't paying any attention at all, I'd take my jeans off and dry them over the radiator.

The second I popped open the button at my waist, he removed his trilby and looked up at me. "Snitch."

"How did he know?" Silly question. Snitch moved like mercury in a maze, fast and fluid.

"So, it *was* another murder?" He watched me begin to wriggle out of the jeans.

"You can look away," I told him. "I want to dry these off."

"I'm a ghost. I see all anyway."

*Was that true? How utterly invasive!* "I don't care! Just look away!"

He popped his trilby back on his head and pulled it down to cover his face again. "Given the number of sticky situations we've shared over the years, I'm surprised you're so bashful."

I hung the jeans up and slipped behind my desk, not in a rush to flash my underwear at him. Safely hidden from his view, I tapped my keyboard until my computer woke up. I intended to scan my emails to see what had come in while I'd been otherwise engaged all day.

"Monkton attended, but at this stage we don't know if it was another murder or not." I frowned. "The thing is, it's a massive coincidence to find two bodies covered in sleeping bags in the space of a few days, isn't it?" I cocked my head, staring in Ezra's direction but not really seeing him. "Monkton suggested that the number of homeless deaths in London is actually quite high. But still … something's not right."

I huffed and turned my attention back to my emails. "I'm not sure what to think at this stage."

"You could do with a look at the pathologist's report," Ezra said.

I nodded, still scanning the senders' list for anything that might be either interesting or lucrative to us as a business. "That's what I was thinking, but now that I'm off the job, there's no way they'll allow me to see the files."

"You used to get on well with Mickey, didn't you?"

I peered across the room. What was on Ezra's mind?

"Yes." We'd appreciated each other's no-nonsense approach to our work.

"So why don't we both go and see him?" Ezra flipped his trilby back, removed his feet from the desk and sat forward.

"Both of us?"

"Yes. You do the banter; I'll take a look at the files when he isn't looking."

I checked the time. "He'll still be at the Packhorse Close scene for a while yet, I should imagine."

"That'll give you time to dry off and warm up."

It sounded like a decent plan. "Won't he be able to see you?" I asked.

"Not if I don't show myself."

I smiled. "It sounds like there are a few advantages to being dead, after all."

"Just as well, isn't it really?" Ezra sniffed. "It's a bit bloomin' boring otherwise!"

CHAPTER 7

The pathology laboratory, attached to The Great London Hospital for Magick and Witchcraft, known as 'HMW', was housed in the basement of one of the older original Victorian hospital buildings. Once upon a time, this grand stucco-fronted building with its enormous windows and tall, mock-Greco columns had been one of the most beautiful buildings in the capital and at the forefront of modern medicine.

These days, because of how massive the wards were, how high the ceilings, how expensive the building was to run and how impossible to heat and clean it was, it had been handed over mainly to research. It housed the morgue and the pathology labs where they'd always been, right in the coldest part of the building, the dead hidden away from Victorian sensitivities.

Funnily enough, I'd felt right at home here from the moment I attended my first post-mortem as a young rookie. The dead had swiftly become my stock-in-trade. Without them, I would never have had a career. All too soon, attending autopsies had simply turned into another avenue of investigation. Whilst viewing ruined bodies in Mickey's—or one of his colleagues'—labs, I found I could remove myself from the emotion of it. Perhaps it sounds trite to say so, but as a detective, once a body is on the slab, you're able to view it objectively as a useful piece of evidence. I took it all in my stride and actually found the process fascinating.

This was in marked contrast to my feelings whenever I was at a scene. I found the scene of the actual crime a forlorn place, devoid of hope, populated only by despair and deep sadness. I always felt choked up when digging around some poor unfortunate victim, searching for the clues that would help me uncover how they'd met their untimely demise.

Therefore, I'd never shied away from what Mickey could share with me.

I opted to use the back entrance that led directly to the morgue. If I'd tried to go in the front, there would be a reception—perhaps closed at this hour, perhaps not, depending how many bodies the place was dealing with—and there would be a security guard with whom I would have had to have a rather difficult conversation about my credentials. By going through the rear door, as long as the security code hadn't changed on the keypad, I would avoid all scrutiny.

I skirted around the building to find a set of unimpressive stone steps camouflaged by some enormous bins marked hazardous waste. I dreaded to think what you might find inside of those. I trotted down the stone steps and entered four digits on the keypad. There was a whirr and a click as the lock released, and I pushed the door open.

Pausing, I glanced behind me, wondering if Ezra was following me or not. *Ha!* I caught myself. *He's a ghost! I probably don't need to hold the door open, do I?* I pulled it closed and made my way along the corridor.

Unlike the labs, where the fluorescents often threatened to burn your corneas out, the lighting in the corridor itself was gentle, and there was little visual stimulation. A few noticeboards and a couple of completely inoffensive paintings of Tower Bridge and Big Ben and such like hung along the walls. It was the smell that really hit you. Disinfectant, formaldehyde and the goddess only knows what other vile and toxic chemicals and cleaners were stored down here. But no matter what, none of those pungent fragrances could mask the underlying perfume of death.

Now that I was safely inside, I felt more confident. I made my way along the corridor to Path Lab Three, the one Mickey inhabited when he wasn't out in the field, knocked, and pushed the door open without giving him the chance to refuse me entry.

There were four tables in here, although only one had a body on it. Mickey, equipped with a bright light and an enormous magnifying glass, was leaning over the corpse, scrutinising the inside of the man's elbow.

"Hey Mickey," I sang, and beamed at him when he looked up.

He raised an eyebrow, pretty much all I could see above his face mask and inside his goggles. "I wondered how long it would be before you showed up in my lab."

I tossed my bag onto his cluttered desk and pulled up a stool. "As if I could stay away from you."

"The thing is—" he started to say, and I heard the weariness in his voice.

I held up my hands in surrender. "Let's save a little time and pretend we've had the conversation where you say you're not allowed to share information with me because I'm no longer with MOWPD, okay?"

"Okay." He bent his head over the body again.

"Is this the guy I found in Packhorse Close this afternoon?" I asked, leaning over to take a look at the face. He was younger than I'd imagined now that I could see him close up.

"Yes. John Doe TT8469."

"They didn't find any ID on him, then?"

"There was nothing in his clothes and nothing in the immediate vicinity when I supervised the removal of the body. If your guys found anything afterwards, they haven't let me know yet."

"I can check that out with Monkton," I said.

Mickey gave me a look. "You've got everyone wrapped around your little finger, I see."

"I'm helping Monkton with his enquiries," I said. It wasn't entirely a lie. He'd been the one who wanted me to visit Cerys. For all I knew, this could be the same case. "They need all the help they can get, now that they're two detectives down." I meant Ezra and me. "Or four if you include Makepeace and Pritchard."

"Yep, pretty short-staffed. Like me. I've got a backlog of cases."

"Sorry to hear that," I sympathised, but pushed on regardless. "So, what can you tell me about this John Doe 8—whatever?"

"TT8469. Not a lot. Cause of death is compression of the throat, though."

"Strangulation?"

"In a manner of speaking." He put down his tools and reached towards me with his gloved hand. "Strangulation generally implies that the victim has been unable to breathe. In this case that was true, however, the vertebrae in the neck were crushed—the hyoid bone and C2 and C3 to be precise—as though the neck had been caught in a vice of some kind."

"Is that even possible?" How could someone end up with their neck in a vice?

"I doubt it. More likely our guy here was strangled by an extremely strong assailant. But I've never seen strangulation injuries on this scale before." He pointed at an X-ray, clipped to a light box. I slid off my stool and went over to turn the light box on so I could study the image. The skull was clearly visible, as were the bones in the shoulder. All I could see in between those two points was a white shadow.

"Ohh-kay? What am I looking at here?" I shrugged in Mickey's direction.

He pulled his lips back in a grimace. "Nice, eh?" He looked back down at John Doe TT8469. "That's not all, though. Come here."

He directed me to the top of the table. "Grab the head and turn with me as I rotate the body. I want to show you something on the back of the neck."

"Alright." I clamped my hands as carefully as I could on the victim's skull. As Mickey turned the shoulders, I moved the head in time.

"There. Do you see?"

I was used to seeing the red flush of rigor mortis and the tell-tale signs of recent violence, but in this case, apart from a round tattoo on the small of his back, the victim had no obvious injuries anywhere except in the area of the neck. I peered closely. Even without Mickey's magnifying glass I could clearly see the indentation of fingers: little red finger-pad shapes, the forefinger and the middle finger the clearest … and the mark of a thumb.

"What do you make of that?" Mickey asked, his eyes sparkling as he looked over John Doe's skinny shoulder at me.

"That seems to indicate strangulation," I said, holding my hands out in front of me to demonstrate to myself. But if I were to strangle Mickey—and to be fair, I had on occasion wanted to do so—my thumbs would meet together at the front and my fingers at the back. I met Mickey's knowing gaze. "That's impossible!"

"The evidence is there before you," said Mickey. "Isn't that what you guys are always nagging me for? Irrefutable evidence. Help me roll him back."

I did so. "So what are we saying?" I asked. "That someone with an enormous hand that could wrap around a man's neck was the attacker? That'll help me narrow down the field."

Mickey nodded. "Pretty much. Either that or it was two people, one on either side, but I can't envisage that scenario."

He couldn't, but my mind went into overdrive.

"Hmm." I slid back on my stool and wrinkled my nose. "Mickey," I wheedled. "You know what I'm going to ask you next, don't you?"

Mickey folded his arms. "You remember that conversation—"

"That we didn't have—"

"—that we should have had. You're no longer MOWPD. You know I can't tell you anything."

I breathed a heavy sigh. "Come on, Mickey! I'm not going to tell anyone you told me."

"Quite right, you're not, because *I'm* not going to tell you anything. It would be more than my job's worth. I haven't even briefed your old boss yet."

I pouted and glared at him across the table. In reply, he only gave me a smug smile. "You're impossible," I grumbled. We were quiet for a moment while I considered my options. What was Ezra up to?

"Alright," I said when it became obvious that Mickey wasn't going to back down. "I tell you what, just answer one small question."

Mickey crooked an eyebrow. "A small question?"

"Yes. A small one. A teeny tiny one." I held up my left hand and indicated half an inch between my thumb and finger.

"Go on." Mickey folded his arms and waited.

"Was DC Makepeace killed in the same way that John Doe TT8-wotsit was?"

"TT8469," Mickey repeated absently. He pressed his lips together for the longest time, considering what to tell me, I suppose. Eventually he gave in. "No."

"No? Then how did he die?"

"Ah-ah!" Mickey waved me away. "You had your *one* small question."

I pressed on. "Do you think both men were killed by the same person?"

"That calls for supposition on the part of the expert witness," Mickey parroted at me. We'd both heard that phrase over and over when giving evidence in court.

"In your opinion—" I persisted.

"Elise, you're like a dog with a bone. I have no idea. None! That's your job. Or it would be your job if you still had it."

"Ouch," I said, and clasped my chest dramatically. "That hurts. I do have a new job though."

He grinned at me. "And you're doing it well, to be fair."

I brightened. "Does that mean you'll tell—"

"No. Now you have to be on your way. I need to get this post-mortem done before DCI Wyld turns up here."

That was the best I was going to do. Well, it was better than nothing, and at least I hadn't fallen out with Mickey over it. "Thank you for your time," I told him. "I owe you a drink."

"You owe me a hangover."

"I'm sure I can make that happen," I winked. "Not

that I'm drinking anymore. I'll just watch you make a fool of yourself. Call me on your next night off."

"You're not drinking? That does surprise me!"

"I'm full of surprises," I laughed and bent down to retrieve my bag.

"There is one thing," Mickey said, his voice becoming serious.

I stood upright, slinging the strap over my shoulder. He gave an almost imperceptible head gesture, and I moved closer to him.

He lowered his voice. "I'm going to tell you this, but I don't want you to repeat it anywhere. Is that understood?"

"Absolutely."

"Help me turn him again."

I did so, and this time Mickey arranged props so the body wouldn't roll of its own accord. He pointed at the tattoo. "See that?"

I had a proper look at it. Approximately three inches in diameter, it turned out not to be a circle but an elaborate labyrinth. The twirls almost looked like miniature hedges. "Nice work," I said.

"It is," Mickey agreed.

"Will you let me take a photo of it?" I asked hopefully, but he looked horrified at the very idea.

"Absolutely not!"

"I've never seen anything like that before."

Mickey sniffed. "Well, I have."

I regarded him curiously. "On another body?" I asked. He must have seen his fill of tattoos over the years.

"Yep. Exactly the same design. *Very* recently."

It dawned on me what he was saying. "Makepeace?"

He nodded. "You didn't hear that from me."

I stared with fresh eyes at the tattoo, trying to memorise it.

"Interesting," I said. "Very interesting."

# CHAPTER 8

No sooner had I closed the door to the hospital basement behind me and climbed the steps than I heard voices, one of them familiar. Monkton Wyld, in the company of one of his sergeants, had arrived to catch poor old Mickey on the hop. I ducked between the large bins, peeking out to watch them pass and feeling slightly guilty that I'd taken up so much of Mickey's time. I was also eager to avoid Monkton seeing me here, thus plunging the pathologist into hot water.

"Have they changed this dratted keycode or something?" I heard Monkton grumbling. It was ever thus; he could never remember security numbers. The problem was, there were always so many of them for us to remember.

"Would you like me to ring Dr O'Mahoney, sir?" the DS, someone I didn't know, asked. "Perhaps he can tell us."

"One more try. Where's Liddell when I need her." I

smirked to hear that. "Oh, here we are!" A buzz and a click, and they were in.

I moved out into the open, startling a nurse who was heading for the car park. She opened her mouth to shriek and I held my hands up to her. "My apologies," I called. "I was looking for something." Before she could respond, I scampered away and kept going until I was out of sight of the hospital.

Under the circle of a streetlamp, I sat on a wall, ignoring the cold damp that swept up to my backside and the prickles of the hedge behind me that caught at my hair. Extracting my notebook and a pen, I rapidly made a sketch of the tattoo as best I could from memory.

"That's rubbish."

Ezra's voice startled me so badly, I nearly tipped backwards.

"In the goddess's name, Ezra!" I tried to steady myself, caught the biro on the wall and sent it spiralling into the hedge behind us. "Now look what you've done." I slipped off my perch, turned and regarded the thick wall of prickles. There was no way I would ever see that Bic again.

"Don't worry," he smiled. "I took a photo." He held up his phone. A ghostly mobile. Presumably, he'd had it in his pocket when he died. He turned the screen so I could see. The image was slightly transparent but good enough. The labyrinthine tattoo.

"Can you send that to me?" I asked, unsure whether a text could be sent from his plane to mine.

"Let's try it," he said, and a few seconds later, my own phone beeped in my bag.

"Clever!" I nodded in satisfaction, deciding I'd forgive him for the loss of my pen.

"I also took the liberty of sneaking a look at Makepeace," Ezra continued.

My mouth dropped open. "How on earth did you manage that?"

"Ghosts can go where private investigators cannot," Ezra said. "I had a look in the fridges until I found his body, and then I—"

"You never!" I closed my eyes and grimaced. "Ezra!"

"I did. Makepeace had this same tattoo, just as Mickey said, but on his wrist, not his back." Ezra twiddled with his phone and showed me the image. "Sorry, I couldn't get a better shot than this. It was dark in there."

"You have no shame," I told him, but secretly I was pleased. He was right. This wasn't a great image, but I could clearly see it was the same tattoo that John Doe had sported. "Anything else?"

"Makepeace's tattoo was recent."

"How recent?"

"Like, the few days before he died kind of recent."

"How could you tell?"

Ezra tapped the inside of his wrist. "When you first have a tattoo, the skin around it can be a bit pink and inflamed."

"And his was?"

"Yep," Ezra confirmed. "Very fresh. I can also tell you that Makepeace did not die the same way as the second body."

"Did you get a look at the records?" I asked. "My understanding was that Mickey didn't know."

"I'm not saying he knows, but I did check out the condition of the body, and I can tell you the neck is intact. He wasn't strangled. Or at least if he was, it wasn't as brutal."

I shuddered. "Well, thanks for checking that detail."

"Anytime." Ezra grinned at me. "So, what's next, boss?"

I studied the image I'd drawn in my notebook. "It would make sense to ask around about tattoo artists, wouldn't it? Just to see if we can find out whose artwork this is. It might help us get a name on our John Doe and give us some insight into what Makepeace was up to. Let's go back and get some shut-eye. We can make a start on that in the morning."

I stuffed my notebook in my bag and we began to walk—well, I walked and Ezra drifted beside me—back in the direction of Tumble Town.

"I didn't know you were such a flirt, Elise," Ezra said.

I cast a sideways glance at him. "Of course you did. I'll flirt with anything with a pulse if it'll get me what I need."

"You're very good at it."

"Thank you."

"Have you and Mickey ever …?" His voice trailed off. Not like Ezra to be bashful.

"No need to be delicate," I said. "The answer is no. But he *is* a good drinking buddy, you know that. You've been on one of our after-work nights out before when we've finished a tough case. He's a lot of fun."

Ezra grinned. "Those were the days. I miss a decent pint of Hoodwinker."

I stopped. "Aren't there any pubs where you are?"

He shrugged. "I haven't found one yet."

"Well, that blows the notion of any kind of utopia out of the window," I said.

"I thought you'd given up drinking?"

"I have, for now." I wiggled my head. "I wanted to give my liver a rest. That's not to say I have forever. Sweet dreams are made of Blue Goblin, if you ask me."

Ezra stuck his tongue out. "I don't know how you can drink that stuff."

"I was kind of hoping that after I passed, I'd prop up a vodka bar for all eternity."

"Sadly, that doesn't appear to happen," Ezra informed me.

I puffed my cheeks out. "Quite frankly, I'm appalled. What kind of an afterlife is that?"

While Wootton transferred the photo of the tattoo from my phone to a file on his laptop, I put the kettle on and made everyone coffee.

It was one of those misty, murky mornings that London is renowned for, where the damp seeps down the alleys and wraps itself around your spine like ice-cold tentacles. I'd left home early and well-prepared for wandering around Tumble Town's copious alleys. I had the robes I'd borrowed from my friend Alfhild Daemonne—I still hadn't managed to get around to buying any of my own, and I hadn't sent hers back—and I had a nice warm jumper on underneath.

The sky, what little I had been able to see of it on my way into work, was slate grey, and the streetlights had remained on. On days like these, most people would have preferred to remain in the comfort of their own homes, perhaps even in bed, but I'd jumped out of bed this morning with my heart singing.

I had an investigation to work on, and boy-oh-boy, I thrived on poking my nose into other people's business.

I hummed happily to myself as I chinked the teaspoon around Snitch's mug. He liked a lot of sugar.

He sat huddled in his filthy old robes, his hair long and lank and his face pale, scowling at me.

"What's up, chuck?" I asked, handing over his brew.

He cradled it, shoulders hunched. "How can you be so bubbly at this time of the morning, DS Liddell?" he asked. "I can barely keep my eyes open."

"DI," I reminded him for the umpteenth time. "You should have gone to bed earlier."

"Earlier?" he questioned. "I haven't been at all yet."

Wootton and I exchanged glances.

"What were you up to all night?" Wootton asked. "Was there a party that I didn't know about?"

Snitch laughed, exposing the gums where his top two teeth should have been. Not a pretty sight. "A party? Don't be daft. No-one invites Snitch to a party."

"I invited you to the pub with me for my birthday, didn't I?" Wootton protested.

"Yeah, you did, you did. But that ain't like a real house party is it? I don't get invited to those."

"Why not?" I asked, barely concealing my sarcasm. "I bet you'd be the life and soul of any gathering."

"Huhuhuhuh," sniggered Snitch. "I think you're pulling me leg, DS Liddell. People think I'd nick stuff."

"Ah," I said. "There is that."

Wootton laughed. "Tell you what, Snitch, if I ever have a party, you'll be the first person I'll invite. Just promise not to walk off with my Witchstation 6."

"Does you 'ave a Witchstation?" Snitch was impressed. "I'd like a go on one of them."

"You should come round," Wootton said. "At the weekend. We'll have a tournament."

"The perfect way to spend your time off," I said. "Not."

Wootton waved the comment away. "Trust me, Grandma, it is." When I rolled my eyes, he added, "Haven't you just moved into your new abode? Maybe you should throw a housewarming party."

"I don't do parties," I replied automatically, then, before he could have another dig about my age, added, "which is not to say I don't like attending parties. I just don't like throwing them. Too much mess to clear up the day after."

The printer began to whirr, spewing forth the tattoo images and a list of the 'official' tattoo shops we'd been able to trace within Tumble Town. It was Snitch's opinion that there were at least double that number of underground tattoo parlours. We had our work cut out for us.

"Are you sure you don't want me to come with you?" Wootton asked as I rolled up the paper and stuffed it into the pocket of my robes. I knew he was hankering to do more investigative work even though, as I'd explained to him numerous times, office research is the backbone of success.

At least in the office he'd stay warm and dry.

"I have Snitch," I said. "Too many of us will look odd."

"You're going to look odd anyway," Wootton muttered under his breath.

I studied Snitch, who was at least six inches shorter than me and as pale as death.

Fair point, Wootton. Fair point.

# CHAPTER 9

"My feet are killing me," Snitch moaned. So far, we'd managed to visit fourteen tattoo parlours. Three of them had been closed, permanently by the look of it, and the others did not recognise the image that I showed them.

Or at least that's what they said.

"You shouldn't have worn stilettos," I quipped, although I had to agree, walking on cobbles for an extended period of time really causes strain on the ankles and knees.

"I'm wearing me walking boots," Snitch replied, obviously missing my joke.

"You should be alright then. What's wrong with you?"

"Yeah, but, see—" He leaned against the wall of the nearest house, twisted his leg and lifted his foot to show me the sole. There was a hole the size of a fifty pence piece in the bottom of his boot. I could clearly see the filthy skin of the underside of his foot.

"Good gracious! Couldn't you have at least worn some socks?"

"I haven't got any that don't have holes in them," he confessed.

"Let me guess," I said, "the holes in your socks match the holes in your boots?"

"Huhuhuhuh. Yeah."

I made a mental note to buy him some boots.

And some socks.

"Where are we off to next?" I scanned the list. "Bewitching Inks? Artisan Lane? Do you know where that is?"

"Yeah, not far." Snitch indicated we go on. "There's another one worth looking at round that way. Wizard Copper's Colour Lounge."

"Where do they dream up these names?" I asked, but I was talking to myself. Snitch had pressed on alone. I hurried to catch him up.

Once upon a time, I had imagined that all the little lanes and alleyways throughout Tumble Town looked very similar. Now I was beginning to learn that each area had a specific character. Artisan Lane was … well, I wouldn't call it upmarket, but it definitely had more of a sense of prosperity than some other neighbourhoods.

The buildings here, while tall and narrow and mid-nineteenth century, were usually well cared for. The paint around the window frames was bright. The window displays were free of dust and more colourful, with a plentiful supply of goods in the windows. This was a stark contrast to somewhere like Cross Lane, where many of the shops had half a dozen items badly displayed in front of a filthy net curtain or a wooden barrier.

I suppose the clue was in the name, 'Artisan Lane'. This was a place to buy arts and crafts of every magickal and mystical persuasion. If you were into paint, felt, wool, sculpture, ink pens, whatever, this was the place for you.

Bewitching Inks looked like virtually every one of the other tattoo parlours we had visited so far today. The lettering on the sign above the window had been painted in gaudy neon rainbow colours. There was a pair of fluorescent flashing signs in the window, proclaiming the store open, and dozens of images from which to choose if you hadn't come prepared with an idea for your artwork.

We stood at the window for a while, scanning the designs. Through the glass I could see three tattoo artists at work, their victims seated in sturdy chairs, reminding me rather of the electric chairs used to execute people in some countries.

"Come on," I said to Snitch. "Let's go in."

We pushed through the door and waited to be noticed. Each of the tattoo artists was concentrating on what they were doing, handling their needles with ease. Eventually, the chap nearest to us looked up and smiled. He lay down his weapon of choice and came to meet us at the reception desk.

He was older than he wanted to be. Wearing black leather trousers, chunky biker boots, a denim jacket with the sleeves cut off, and sporting an impressive green and blue mohawk along with dozens and dozens of intricate and colourful tattoos and a face full of piercings. He was exactly the sort of person I'd imagine working in a tattoo parlour. He'd seen a lot of sun too—somewhere other than Tumble Town, I could only imagine—for his skin was as tanned as leather and his face deeply and prematurely lined.

"Alright, love?" He looked me up and down. "What'ya after? I can fit you in after Doris 'ere. 'E won't be long."

I glanced over at the enormous man in the artist's chair, with a huge and powerful arm exposed. *He was called Doris?*

"I'm not after a tattoo, thank you," I replied, keeping it polite as Snitch shifted from foot to foot beside me.

"That's a shame." Mohawk Man winked at me. Nope, I wasn't in a rush to reveal any part of my body to him.

"Maybe another time." I fished the image of the tattoo out of my pocket. "I just need a moment of your time. I was wondering if you had ever given someone a tattoo like this?"

He took the image from me and scanned it. "Nice bit of artistry that." He handed it back to me. "Not mine, though."

"Would it be anything your colleagues have worked on?" I gestured at the other two tattoo artists, one man and one woman, both in their twenties.

"Nah."

"How can you be so certain?" I asked, curious as to why he hadn't shown the picture to them and wondering if he was being deliberately evasive.

"I'd know their art anywhere, and this just isn't their style." He gave me a hard look.

I wasn't fazed. I studied the image again, myself. "So you can tell there is some kind of style to this?"

"Everyone has their own style, love." He leaned a little too close to me. "See the swirls there?" He pointed at a section of the drawing I had never considered before. "Nice, that is. Neat work. Precise."

"Would you know who might do work like this?" I asked, hopeful that as he was now being so helpful, he wouldn't mind sharing information.

He glanced at Snitch. "Nah," he said.

I waited a few beats, optimistic he would reconsider. He didn't.

"Alright." I shoved the picture back in the pocket of my robes. "Thanks so much for your time."

"Yeah, well, y'know," he shrugged, "happy to help. If you ever do want some ink doing, or whatever?"

There would definitely be no 'whatever'.

"You'll be the first one I approach," I promised him.

I smiled and nodded, and together with Snitch, ventured outside onto the street. Snitch mock-shivered.

"It's not that cold," I told him. "It's almost summer. Imagine if we were doing this in January!"

"It is when you have no soles," he reminded me. I hadn't forgotten though. How could I, when he kept hopping from foot to foot?

"Where shall we go next?" I asked him, reaching for the list again. I wouldn't say I'm a slavedriver, but I do like to get the work done.

Snitch's face crumpled. I was afraid he was about to burst into tears. "I'm hungry."

"I'll buy you a nice hot pie, if you like?" I offered. It was the least I could do.

Snitch's face lit up. "From Betty's?"

I looked around doubtfully. "We've come a long way from Tudor Lane. There must be a bakery closer than Betty's."

"You can't beat Betty's," Snitch said, lifting his chin.

"One more tattoo parlour and then—"

"I tell you what …" Snitch smiled his toothless smile at me, his eyes sly. I already didn't like what he was going to suggest. "You go on to the next one by yourself —it's not as though you need me—and I'll nip back to Betty's and get us a pie each."

"It's a long way—"

"I know a shortcut," Snitch reassured me. "I won't be long."

"Okay, if you're sure." I checked my list. "The next tattoo parlour is on Quartz Cross Square."

"Sound!" Snitch nodded and pointed back the way we'd come. "Go back there, hang a left and take the third right. You can't miss it. I'll meet you there."

"Alright."

He stood and stared at me, not going anywhere.

I stared back at him. Waiting.

We stared at each other.

"It's your treat," he reminded me.

"Oh! That's right." I fumbled for some cash and handed it over to him. "Bring me back the change," I told him as though he were an eight-year-old.

"Will do!" With that he darted away, faster than I'd seen him move all morning.

I replaced my purse and the list and was about to head off in the direction Snitch had indicated, when the door of Bewitching Inks was pulled open behind me. I stepped back to make way for Doris. He looked a little pale, clutching his arm at the elbow, his shoulder no doubt smarting.

I nodded as he walked past me, but he barely even noticed me.

Such is the way of Tumble Town.

He was followed out by Mohawk Man, who stood on the top step, regarding me thoughtfully.

"Still 'ere?" he asked.

"Just getting my bearings," I told him.

"Are you sure you don't want some ink? I'm free now."

I shook my head and smiled. Mohawk Man was persistent, I'd give him that. "Nah," I said, echoing the way he spoke, just for my own amusement really.

"Alright, girl." He sniffed and looked up and down the lane. Seeing it all clear, he closed the shop door and hustled right up close to me.

"Where's your friend gone?"

"To grab a spot of lunch." I gave Mohawk Man a little dead-eye. I hardly needed Snitch of all people to protect me—as Mohawk Man would find out if he laid a finger on me.

He curled his lip as though I smelt disagreeable and brought his face closer to mine. It took all my self-control not to knee him in the nuts.

"I know a tattoo place you should try," he whispered.

I blinked in surprise. Before I could ask where, he lifted a finger and held it to my lips. I could discern the tangy scent of chemicals from his inks. I resisted the urge to reach up and break the digit off.

"Culpeper's. Buckingham Place."

"That sounds rather grand," I said.

"It isn't." He held my gaze, his eyes hooded. "You'll need to tread carefully."

"I don't know where—"

"Follow the lane as it curls around here. To your left, two hundred yards maybe, you'll see some steps. A *lot* of steps. Go up and turn right. It's a lane squashed between two rows of houses."

I nodded.

He hadn't finished. "It's dark, it's dingy and it's dangerous. Do your business and get out."

"Thank you."

"Don't mention my name. I haven't seen you. I don't know you."

With that, he turned on his heel and climbed back into the shop, closing the door so violently the glass rattled.

That left me in a quandary. I'd told Snitch I would meet him at Quartz Cross Square. But this was my first potential lead. I simply couldn't afford not to follow it up.

I'd be quick. It would take ages for Snitch to get to Betty's.

I set off the way that Mohawk Man had suggested.

CHAPTER 10

I had never really noticed that Tumble Town was hilly before. Like most of London, it had seemed relatively flat to me and yet, within twenty yards of Bewitching Inks, the path started to drop down quite steeply as it curled around. I followed the bend, glad of my sturdy boots as the descent became trickier. I hurried past a toy shop and an art gallery, a well-stocked butcher—feathery pheasants hanging from hooks in the window—a wand shop and a rather enchanting shop with a wooden front carved to resemble trees. It turned out to be selling robes.

I made a mental note to visit that one and have some made up.

I almost missed the entrance to the steps on my left, thanks to the ivy that stretched between the buildings here and camouflaged the opening. I pushed through and found an ancient flight of roughly hewn stone risers, heavily worn over time. Moss had gathered at the side of each step, but the central path was clear. *I might* not know of the existence of this place, but clearly, others did.

The steps stretched away into the darkness. I peered doubtfully up into the gloom, then whisked out my wand and lit the tip. "*Illuminate.*"

The light illuminated a small street sign to my left, a couple of feet above my head. Providence Steps. Now I could see at least about eight feet in front of me, I began to climb.

And therein lay another surprise. I considered myself relatively fit. While I'd been serving with the MOWPD, I'd visited the gym several times a week. You never knew when you'd have to chase a runaway suspect. Since Ezra's death I'd been less active, but I'd still managed to get out for a run every few days. After moving to Tumble Town, I'd preferred to do that in the daylight hours. The nights were alive with strange folk and I never felt entirely safe.

But these steps? They seemed to go on forever. I found myself sucking in oxygen as though I were climbing Everest. And the higher I ascended, the shallower the steps became—until what had been a riser of ten or so inches at the bottom of this peculiar mountain now became around two inches, and I was working harder than ever.

I took a pause and leaned against the damp wall of the building to my left to catch my breath. Behind me, someone cleared their throat. I was so startled I nearly fell backwards onto them. I spun about, and a little old woman, her back hunched and a scarf tied around her head and knotted under her chin, waited for me to move.

"I'm so sorry!" I said. I'd had no idea I was being followed. I pressed my back against the wall so she could climb past me.

She did so without so much as looking at me or saying a word. She simply carried on up and disappeared out of my sight, not breaking a sweat and certainly not breathing as heavily as me.

"Well … fancy," I panted. Once I had my breath back, I began to climb again.

It took an age, but just when I thought I would collapse from over-exertion, I came to an opening on my right between two rows of one- and two-storey terraced dwellings, ramshackle and higgledy-piggledy like something you might find in a Devonshire coastal town. This time, the street sign attached to the nearest building confirmed that this was Buckingham Place.

*Really?*

I turned back to peer up the steps. They carried on ahead of me. Up, up and into the distance. Way above me I thought I saw a light of some kind, but I had no intention of climbing any further to investigate. The effort would probably kill me. Mind made up, Snitch all but forgotten, I took the turning on the right and moved into one of the dingiest alleys Tumble Town had thus far shown me.

The teeny-weeny houses were crowded together and, like much of Tumble Town, the front doors opened straight out onto the street. The front windows faced those of the house opposite. I could have trailed a hand against a building on each side of the walkway—that's how close they were—but I didn't because … well, they were filthy. Plaster crumbled from the brickwork, the wooden window frames were chipped, the paint peeling, the windows thick with grime and the chimneys emitted a thick, sooty smoke that coated your lungs every time you took a breath in.

The path started to descend—having climbed one hill, it looked like I was going back down it—but fortunately there were no more steps to navigate. In the smog-ridden gloom of Buckingham Place, I had a feeling I would have probably missed my step and rolled to the bottom, fracturing my skull and breaking a few ribs and fingers along the way.

Culpeper's? That's what I was looking for? There didn't appear to be any shops here at all.

I scanned the buildings as I walked until I spotted something slightly different to the others in its general proximity. The glow from a larger window. It pulled me in. I stopped directly in front of it. The building was an odd green colour, like someone had mixed forest green with battleship grey, although it certainly hadn't been painted recently. Probably not in about fifty years. The window had a boxed-in display area, making it impossible to see inside the shop—if that's what it was—and was downlit. But the only object on display was a single hookah pipe.

I had seen many of these over the years. In fact, I'd visited a sheesha bar with a couple of my ex-colleagues on a social night out, and, in my younger days on the beat, I'd been involved in busting one such bar in

Camden. But I don't think I'd ever seen a pipe as pretty as this one. The glass water bowl, or vase, was hand-blown and beautifully decorated in swirling rainbow colours, and the neckpiece had been intricately painted with an oriental design: tiny, complex and strangely fascinating. I stood for a while, trying to discern the shapes. Little people. Pandas. Gold temples. Lions.

So, what was this place? I tipped my head back to have a look at the faded, painted sign above the window. It read only '*Culpeper's. Est. 1852*'.

*Keep it in the family, eh?*

I stepped sideways to stand in front of the door and hesitated. There was no glass in the door; it was solid wood. As with the window, there was no clue as to what I would find inside. No hint at whether I should knock or simply step inside.

What if I walked straight into someone's living room?

Decision time. I couldn't wait outside all day. I lifted my hand and tapped with my knuckles. Rat-a-tat-tat! The police officer's knock. I waited for a couple of beats, then turned the big old-fashioned brass knob and pushed the door. It swung inwards without so much as a creak, opening into a small, dark room, perhaps ten feet wide and twelve deep.

I stepped inside, imagining the lights would be auto-matic, perhaps motion sensors, and that they would blink on, but nothing occurred to alleviate the gloom. I squinted into the darkness. There was a tall, heavily polished counter at one end, and a door leading to a back room or the rest of the house perhaps, but apart from that, and another sign similar to the one hanging above the window outside, nothing.

No decoration. No paintings. No artwork. No more hookah pipes.

Nothing on the counter. Nothing behind the counter. No hint of what this place was at all.

I glanced around, my heart beating a little harder and faster, senses working overtime. I still had my wand in my hand. I just needed to remain alert.

"Mmm? If you could close the door."

I caught my breath.

"The door?" A male voice. Quiet and pinched. Nasal. Upmarket. Impatient.

"Sorry," I replied automatically and closed the door behind me, plunging the room into pitch black. There was a scratch and a hiss, and the man lit a match. He stood in the far-right corner, behind the counter. Perhaps he'd been there all the time. I don't know.

I couldn't see his face, but his body shape was thin and angular and he was wearing a hat … a top hat, rather like something Hattie would make but much less interesting. This one was plain black and entirely in keeping with the whole Dickensian feel of the place.

He used his match to light a gas lamp. I don't think I had ever seen one of those in operation before. Like the hookah pipe, it had beautifully coloured handblown glass. The light flared, and I momentarily caught sight of his face: a neatly trimmed moustache and beard and sallow skin—then he turned the gas down and his features were lost to the shadows.

"Mmm?" he said, and I realised this was one of his

tics. He started most of his utterances with the sound, like a car revving its engine before the clutch is released. "May I be of assistance?" He stretched his words out as though he was savouring each and every letter.

"Good afternoon," I replied, keeping my voice light and breezy but professional too. "I do hope I haven't disturbed you. I have been making some enquiries at tattoo parlours, and someone recommended Culpeper's." I looked around meaningfully. "I fear I may have come to the wrong place."

The man regarded me silently for some time. I waited, always patient; Ezra had schooled me in this technique a long time before.

"Who recommended us?" The man finally broke the silence.

"I forget his name," I lied. Not that I'd ever known Mohawk Man's name, but I'd given a silent promise not to spill the beans. "You *are* a tattoo artist, are you?"

"Mmm? I have many skills."

He wasn't being particularly forthcoming. I hoped I wasn't wasting my time.

"Perfect," I smiled. Perfectly unforthcoming, in fact. "I'm Elise Liddell," I told him, stepping closer to the counter. "And you are?"

"Mmm-mister Culpeper."

"Of course." I rummaged in my robes for the image of the tattoo and lay the paper on the counter between us, smoothing it out because it had become a little wrinkled from all the handling. "I'm looking for an artist who can create this."

Mr Culpeper shifted in the shadows and, while I still

couldn't see his face, the tilt of his top hat suggested his head was angled down. He was studying the image, but he didn't say anything.

I pressed on. "Is this something you could do?"

There followed another drawn-out silence. I sensed him sizing me up.

"No," he said eventually. Emotionless.

I remained silent.

"Mmm? Who sent you here?" I heard the faintest hint of irritation in his tone. He masked it well.

"I'm sorry," I said. "I've visited so many places this morning looking for the artist of this tattoo, and you were added to the list."

"Mmm? Where did you get this image?"

So far, nobody had asked me that question. I found it interesting that Mr Culpeper wanted to know. It seemed to me that there was more to him than met the eye. Not that my eye was being met by very much, though. He stubbornly remained in the shadows. It was difficult for me to read him, although that in itself told me more than he might have imagined.

"I saw it on a corpse," I told him, deciding to play it straight.

Another lengthy pause.

"Mmm? Are you the police?"

"No." I didn't elucidate. "Did you create this?"

"Mmmmmm?" The sound drifted away as though he had run out of steam.

"Do you know who did?"

This time he didn't answer at all. There was no clock in this strangely minimalist room, but in my head I could clearly hear one ticking. I was getting absolutely nowhere but I was certain Mr Culpeper knew more than he was letting on.

"Mmm? I have to close now," he said, and he leaned forward a little. His eyes glittered as he twiddled with the gas lamp.

"If I could just ask—"

The room went dark. "Good day to you, Ms Liddell." His voice drifted out of the shadows.

There came a click behind me. I spun around. The front door opened of its own accord and swung silently inwards. "Good day to you," he repeated.

Although disgruntled, I realised there was nothing else for it but to leave. I didn't have anything useful to work with, but I'd certainly dig into Mr Culpeper's background.

"Good day," I said, and stepped reluctantly out into Buckingham Place. The door closed behind me, locking by itself. It reminded me of my visit to Mr Kephisto's book shop in Devon.

I climbed the hill back the way I'd come until I found myself at the steps. I waited to let a little old woman, slightly hunched, a headscarf knotted beneath her chin, pass me on her climb to the top. She didn't say anything, but she looked oddly familiar. I peered after her. It couldn't be the same one I'd seen earlier, surely?

I illuminated my wand, carrying it in my right hand, my left hand stretched out to steady myself against the uneven wall at the side of me. Wishing for a railing, I carefully began the descent. The steps were uneven, slightly slippery. Because I was concentrating so hard on where I was placing my feet, I almost didn't see the figure that loomed in front of me hurrying up the steps towards me until it was too late. I gasped in shock as we almost collided. Another woman. Another knotted headscarf.

*The same one?*

How could that be?

She levelled a malevolent glare my way and pushed past me, hard enough to knock me slightly off balance.

"No need for that," I called to her retreating back as I clutched at the brickwork, plaster crumbling beneath my fingers. But she wasn't remotely interested in me or my protestation. She kept right on going, not looking back.

I huffed in annoyance and continued down the steps. I hadn't gone far when I heard a scuffling noise behind me, followed by the sound of small pieces of rock or pebbles tumbling down the steps. I half-turned and my vision was filled by a rush of black as something pushed past me from behind and enveloped me in its darkness. I had a flash of a skeletally thin face, as pale as the moon, transparent eyes, red stubble. I stumbled forwards, my foot searching for a step that should have been there but wasn't. I couldn't see. Completely blind, I spiralled my arms. Gravity pulled at me and I began to fall. I braced myself as the air rushed around me. My head dropped forwards and my weight shifted. I threw my arms out in front of me, desperate to protect my head and neck from the painful impact that would follow.

But then a hand reached out from the shadows. I

caught a brief glimpse of nails bruised and blackened before it grabbed my wrist in a painfully tight hold and hauled me backwards. My feet scrambled at the ground and I found purchase. I settled my weight solidly on a step, balanced there, my breathing ragged, my heart thumping, my vision grey at the edges.

I looked down at the hand that had curled around my wrist. I couldn't see what it was attached to and, even as I watched, the fingers peeled away and disappeared into the shadows.

"Mmm?"

I gasped and turned about, but there was nothing to see.

No-one there.

Shaking, I resumed the descent, my body half-turned to watch out for assailants behind me as well as in front. I didn't relax until I made it back onto Artisan Lane.

# CHAPTER 11

"I didn't see Mr Culpeper's hands, so I can't know for certain that it was him who saved me from falling down the steps," I repeated for the third time. I'd staggered back to the office and found Snitch had arrived a few minutes before, alarmed by my no-show at Quartz Cross Square.

Ezra was listening to my story, and Hattie was dabbing at a bump and cut on my brow with a huge wad of cotton wool.

"But from what you've said, it must have been him." Wootton plonked a mug of coffee in front of me. I picked it up and cupped my hands around it gratefully. The encounter had left me feeling a little shocked and cold. Coffee would sort me out, although a shot of Blue Goblin would not have gone amiss.

"But it wasn't all of him," I said. "Just one hand. How bizarre is that?"

"I don't think it's that bizarre," Snitch said. His face

was a picture of woe. "I am so sorry, DS Liddell. I really shouldn't have left you alone, but—"

"It's fine."

"I was hungry and my feet were aching—" he wailed.

"Snitch! Don't worry about it. These things happen." I sought to reassure him, although he had the look of a man who expected to go to the noose at any moment.

Hattie dabbed my brow dry and, before I could protest, clamped a sticking plaster in place, pressing it down firmly with the palm of her hand.

"Ow!"

"Sorry, dearie. All done now." Hattie turned to Snitch. "Don't you worry, lad. She'll live."

"Nice plaster, Hattie," Wootton chortled, and I reached up to feel the edges. It was half the size of a football pitch.

"Is that really necessary?" I grumbled.

"It's all I have at the moment," Hattie told me and disposed of her 'medical kit'—something that comprised of a bag of pleated cotton wool, some TCP and a mug without a handle she was using in lieu of a bowl.

"It's the little white rabbits on it that are most fetching," Wootton chuckled.

"Is it an Alice in Wonderland band-aid?" I asked.

"Yes, a prized part of my bathroom cabinet, so I hope you're grateful." That shut me up. I sipped at my coffee. It had sugar in it. I didn't normally take sugar, but this afternoon I was grateful for it.

"I think if you're going to go to any more of these

tattoo parlours, it would be best if I came along," Ezra said.

"Would there be any point?" I asked him. "You're not a physical being anymore. You couldn't have fought my attacker off."

"And yet, from what you've described, it wasn't a person who attacked you," he was quick to point out.

"It all happened so fast." I rubbed my forehead, the swelling tender beneath the dressing. "I don't even remember banging my head, but I must have done."

"Do you think it was the woman who passed you who pushed you?" Wootton asked. "I mean, you gave her some lip, right?"

"I didn't give her any lip." I frowned at him. "Not really." I thought back, remembering how she had receded from my view. It hadn't looked like she was going to rush down and assault me. "No. I don't think it was her. Besides, whoever it was—"

I closed my eyes, momentarily taking myself back to the frightening moment on the steps. The way the world had suddenly turned black as though someone had thrown a cloak over my head. The rush of air. The face. Gaunt features. Transparent eyes—

My breath hitched noisily as I opened my eyes. The others stared at me. Ezra with interest, the others warily.

"In the factory." I breathed out and swivelled my head to gaze out of the window. The others followed my gaze. What light there had been today was failing fast. I stood and made my way over to the window, still cradling my coffee. I regarded the factory windows opposite. Not so long ago, I would have been able to peer out of my windows and into the deserted building opposite, but now even the windows on the top floor had been boarded up.

"What's in the factory?" Wootton came to stand next to me.

"That's where I saw that face before. The man who attacked me then also attacked me on the steps up to Buckingham Place. He was also the man I saw Cerys with in the pub that time. What was it called? The Nautical Mile."

"I thought the man you saw Cerys with had substance," Ezra said. "From the way you described the man who attacked you in the factory and the one on the steps this afternoon, I had the impression he was more …"

"Ephemeral," I finished for him. "You're right. It's almost as though he exists on both planes." I looked at Snitch. "Is that possible?" I asked him. "Are there beings like that in Tumble Town?"

"Or anywhere?" Wootton added.

Snitch grimaced. "I'm hardly the expert you need here, DS Liddell."

"But you've lived here your whole life—"

"So have I!" Hattie protested.

"And me," Wootton nodded.

"Okay, okay." I gestured around at everyone with my mug, the coffee swishing dangerously close to the rim and spilling on the floor. I ignored it, but Hattie was quick to mop it up with a handful of cotton wool. "I'm just thinking, you know, that Snitch might have his ear a little closer to the ground than the rest of us."

Snitch seemed to like that because he offered me his gappy smile.

"But I'm willing to hear from anyone." I returned to my desk and drained my drink in one.

"There's the Shadow People," Snitch ventured.

"But Shadow People don't have any substance," Wootton argued. "Not ever."

"They are just shadows," Hattie agreed.

"Are they? What is a shadow? Do they have any kind of form?" I looked around at a sea of blank faces. "Who are they? Where do they come from?" I flicked on my computer as though I imagined I could just go to Google and find out.

"I don't think anyone knows," Wootton said.

Snitch nodded his agreement. "It's true. They've just always been here. Like always, always."

"Do they do anything?" I asked. "I mean … do they mug people or what?"

"Not everyone in Tumble Town is a criminal!" Hattie sounded most put out.

Just *most* people, I thought. Around ninety per cent, probably. But perhaps I was being unkind.

"All the Shadow People seem to do is laugh," said Snitch.

"Not all of them laugh," Wootton disagreed. "Some of them can be downright creepy."

"Laugh," I repeated. It wasn't a question. What Snitch said was true. There were plenty of them who giggled from the sidelines. And they giggled because they found things funny. And they found things funny because they were always listening and always watching. There was probably nowhere in Tumble Town, except the inside of people's dwellings—and perhaps not even there—where the Shadow People couldn't be located.

The most unnerving thing about them was that you would never know they were there until they laughed or unexpectedly said something.

"Wow," I said. It had suddenly occurred to me that if you needed to know anything at all about the goings-on in Tumble Town, the Shadow People would be the ones to ask.

"What's on your mind, boss?" Ezra regarded me knowingly.

"Apart from a huge bump," Wootton added, tittering at his own joke.

I clapped my hands. "Let's see what we can find out about Mr Culpeper first of all." I pointed my finger at Wootton and he nodded. "Snitch and Ezra, why don't you guys see if there's any possibility we could get a Shadow Person to actually talk to us?"

Snitch looked horrified. "How—?"

"I have absolutely no idea," I said. "Maybe wander around the area until you hear one and then see if they'll answer you when you talk to them?"

"What do you want me to do?" Hattie asked.

"You could put the kettle on again?" I asked, ever hopeful.

With the exception of Hattie, who had forgone tea-making duties in order to complete a hat order for a client in Australia, we reconvened just after seven. I wouldn't normally have the office open that late, but we had stayed on because, it seemed to me, we were getting nowhere.

Ezra had returned without Snitch, who had taken fright and bolted apparently. "And without him, I had no luck at all. It was just no good," Ezra told me. "I couldn't get close to them unless I was with Snitch."

"How do you mean?" I queried.

"When I was alone, I could never hear them. If I joined forces with Snitch, we would periodically come across them and I'd hear them then."

"That's odd," I said. "You're saying that they don't react around ghosts?"

"I'd always assumed they *were* ghosts, but that may not be the case," Ezra confirmed. "But I definitely can't hear them anymore. Not when I'm alone."

"And Snitch? Did he try and talk to them?"

"He did but couldn't get any sense out of them."

I sighed. "Oh." It had been a good idea. Misguided perhaps, but worth trying.

Wootton swung back on his chair. I didn't like him doing that; I was always frightened he was going to tumble out of the window, but I daren't say anything because he'd only have called me Grandma.

"I've drawn a similar blank with our Mr Culpeper," he announced.

I slumped back in my seat. "You can't have. Everyone leaves a trace somewhere."

Wootton swung his computer screen around so that Ezra and I could see, then angled his chair so that he could too. "Right, here's what I have."

He clicked his keyboard and located an image. "This is from the British Newspaper Archive online, from a newspaper called *The Tumble Globe*, now defunct. It announced the opening of Mr Culpeper's Bazaar of Oriental Curiosities way back in 1852. April the twenty-seventh, to be exact."

"And what was the Bazaar of Oriental Curiosities?" I wanted to know. "Antiques? Imports?"

"The article doesn't specify, and back then there were no photographs, of course. Buckingham Place was an up-and-coming area at the time, not far from Artisan Lane. Artisan Lane itself had been established for a couple of centuries, but it was known for being cheap. All the trendy young bohemian Victorian paranormals, writers and artists and what have you, used to hang out there, apparently. The article talks more about the growth of free enterprise and workshops in the area, but there is a rather fetching illustration of Mr Culpeper himself."

I pushed myself out of my chair so I could get a closer look at the picture. "The apple hasn't fallen far from the tree there," I marvelled. "My Mr Culpeper looked like that, but with a beard." I studied the image. "What relation would this Mr Culpeper be to my Mr Culpeper?" I tried to work out the generations. "Great-great-grandfather? Great-great-great?" I gave up.

"That in itself is interesting," Wootton said. "I've had a good old trawl through the registers of births, deaths and marriages, and I can find a birth record in the Tumble Town parish register that may be him." He clicked into a new window and I stared down at a faded birth record, highlighted in yellow, written in an almost illegible scrawl. "William Thomas Culpeper, born 1801 to Mary Culpeper nee Swanidge and William Edward Culpeper, artist."

Wootton folded his arms. "But after that, the trail goes cold. There's no marriage record that I can find and no death record. He doesn't show up in any census—although I suppose that's not unusual for this part of London. However, I *can* find the shop on all sorts of business registers, right through to the present day."

"So, Culpeper's as a business has existed since 1852?" Ezra asked. "And always as a going concern?"

Wootton nodded. "Yep. But there's no mention of the original Mr Culpeper in any of the cemetery records, so he wasn't buried in Tumble Town either."

"He must have retired to the country," Ezra said. "A lot of people do it."

"What about other Culpepers? It's not against the realms of possibility that he had a son and didn't register him, is it?" I asked.

"He might even have had a son out of wedlock," Ezra suggested.

"Or," I thought aloud, "perhaps he handed the business down to a close relative. A nephew or someone?"

"I can't find any trace of any other Culpepers apart from a small batch who live over on Deadman's Wharf. They are sailors and carpenters, and there doesn't appear to be any link between them and our Mr Culpeper."

"What about more recently?" I asked.

"You reckoned your Mr Culpeper was what? About fifty years old?" Wootton asked.

I nodded. "Thereabouts, yes. Difficult to tell given he was hiding in the shadows most of the time."

"I promise, I've searched through every decade and every record I have access to, and I've found nothing. No discernible relatives, either in Tumble Town or out of it."

I screwed my nose up. "That's odd."

"Obviously there are other Culpepers dotted around the UK and beyond," Wootton said, and a look of dread passed over his face. He knew what I was going to say next.

"Check them all out," I said.

Ezra laughed at Wootton's curled lip. "You want to be a detective, sunshine. That means doing the donkey work."

"Yeah, but—" Wootton began to protest.

"Believe me, it doesn't get any better as you go through your career!" I nodded at my young apprentice, then turned to wink at Ezra. "How many hours did we used to put into database searches on some of our cases?"

"It felt like years," Ezra said. "Decades, even. And back when I started, databases were drawers full of handwritten and filed cards."

"That's no consolation," Wootton grumbled.

Ezra held a finger up. "You know, there's always the

possibility that the business is being handed down by people who are no relation and have simply taken the name Culpeper."

"That's true," I said, nodding at Wootton. "Why don't you see what you can find out about name changes?"

"I'll add it to my list," Wootton said, and now he sounded resigned.

I reached over and scrolled through Wootton's windows until I came back to the one from *The Tumble Globe*. "It strikes me though, that for someone who isn't directly related to the original Mr Culpeper, my Mr Culpeper looks very similar. They could almost be brothers."

"Maybe it's the same chap," Wootton said and drew his keyboard closer so he could resume work.

"Ha!" I laughed. "Yeah, maybe."

# CHAPTER 12

It had been a long day and my forehead was throbbing. At around twenty to nine I decided to lock up the office and head home. Visions of a hot bath to ease my aches and pains before retiring to bed before midnight cheered me up immensely.

"I could walk you back," Ezra offered but, tempted as I was, I decided to go alone. I hadn't been a resident of Tumble Town for long, but I already realised that the more people began to recognise me around the streets on my daily commute between my office and Peach-stone Market, the less likely they were to give me any trouble.

"Don't worry, I'm not going to make any detours," I told him, grabbing my bag and slinging it over my shoulder. "I'll be perfectly safe."

Outside, the night was unusually clear. Moonlight filtered between the narrow gaps between the roofs of the buildings on Tudor Lane. I remembered the higgledy-piggledy low rise of the houses in Buckingham

Place in marked contrast to these old Elizabethan and Georgian structures and, lost in thought, I almost ignored Charles Lynch standing outside The Pig and Pepper, taking the air.

Or escaping his clientele.

Or something.

"What's that on yer 'ead?" he asked without preamble.

"And a very good evening to you," I said.

Someone in the shadows tittered. "Manners cost nothing," they said. Another unseen being in an adjacent doorway chuckled in response. I turned about quickly but there was no-one to see.

"Hello?" I called, eager to see if they would talk to me.

"Ignore them." Charles aimed a kick at nothing in particular. "Be orf wiv ya!" he hollered, and the giggles faded away. "You been in the wars or something?" He pointed at my forehead.

"Something like that, yes." I gestured into the dark doorway of the building next to us. "What do you know about the people in the shadows?"

"What's there to know?" he shrugged. "They've always been there."

"Are they the same ones? Do they come and go?"

Charles folded his thick arms across his chest. "Y'know what your problem is, Orficer?"

I set my jaw and waited.

"Ya think too darn much. Always wantin' to know stuff. Always askin' yer questions. Some people, not me like, but some … they'd call it prying."

"Is that right?"

"Yeah, it is." Charles looked pleased with himself like he'd just solved a particularly thorny problem. "You need to chill out a bit. 'Ave a drink. Relax."

"You're probably right," I said, controlling the urge to stomp on his toe. "Maybe I should venture into your fine establishment and check out your stock of Blue Goblin."

He stepped in front of his open door. "We wouldn't want to be upsetting my regular punters for no good reason now, would we?"

I peered over his shoulder, wondering who he had inside he wanted to protect. "Something going on you don't want me to know about, Charles?" I asked.

"Not at all, not at all," he said, but he didn't move.

"Don't worry," I told him. "I'm after an early night, not a skinful, so some other time."

I winked and walked away.

He let me go, but after a dozen steps he called after me. "I used to recognise one of them."

I stopped and looked around, not instantly sure what he was referring to. "Who?"

"One of the Shadow People," he explained. "Not recognise, like. Never saw her face. But it was a woman. And I came to recognise the voice cos it sounded like my old nan."

I walked back to him. "Was it your nan?"

"Like a ghost, you mean? Nah. I see some ghosts. I see your Ezra." He nodded, his eyes knowing. "She weren't no ghost, this voice. Not my nan's ghost anyway, cos she was still alive for a while. At the same time, like. Y'know?"

"What happened to the voice?" I asked, confused.

"I stopped hearing her a few years back. Maybe she went to plague someone else. Maybe she'll come back again. Maybe I went deaf. Who knows?"

"Who knows, indeed." I nodded and waved my hand at him as I walked away. Could the Shadow People have a lifespan of some kind?

Food for thought.

Cross Lane is Tumble Town's main conduit. If you want to get anywhere, Cross Lane is the place to start. I therefore headed that way, intending to walk in the opposite direction to Celestial Street in the north, towards the river. Eventually, I would simply hang a left and then a right, another left and another right and shortly find myself on the parameters of Peachstone Market.

The whole journey should have taken eleven minutes. I knew that because I'd timed it. Eleven short minutes between me and a hot bath and my comfy bed. Perhaps I'd even phone my friend George Gilchrist for a natter.

That was the plan.

Unfortunately, as I began to walk along the narrow confines of Cross Lane, half an ear tuned in to listen for Shadow People, I caught the now-familiar bright flash that heralded the appearance of the white rabbit.

I stopped and stared at it.

Cross Lane was 'busy', in the relative way that Tumble Town sometimes can be. People shifted quietly on the periphery of my vision. Some, wearing cloaks or pointed hats, walked more boldly, either towards me or past me, but none of them ever made eye contact. I could sense life all around me, but to all intents and purposes, I was alone there, with the white rabbit relaxed on its haunches, staring up at me with its beautiful brown eyes.

"Not tonight," I told it, because I already thought I knew what its appearance would herald. "I have plans."

It twitched its nose in response.

I breathed out heavily, my image of a relaxing evening vanishing from my mind with a poof, as though someone had popped my thought balloon.

"It's cruel and unnecessary," I grumbled. The rabbit turned away and hopped a few feet down Cross Lane before peering back to make sure I was following.

"Lead on, Macfluff," I said.

It skipped away, and I followed it easily enough. There was plenty of light and it was a dry evening. I angled myself sideways whenever I met anyone walking towards me, patting my handbag to reassure myself it was safe, careful not to show much interest in anyone and quite frankly, amazed that no-one paid any attention to the rabbit. But they didn't, and it had eyes only for me.

Tonight, it led me along a route that seemed familiar, down Cross Lane at a brisk pace. Finally, it paused, glanced back and shot off to the right. I drew level with the turning and lifted my head to survey the street sign.

Packhorse Close.

Where I'd found the second body.

Without a thought for my own safety, I hurried after the rabbit while rummaging in my bag for my mobile. I was going to have to call this in, and the sooner that was taken care of, the sooner I'd be able to get home.

I heard a scuffle up ahead and broke into a run, abandoning the search for my phone and settling on my wand instead. I extended it in front of me as I observed a couple of shapes in the distance. As I gained ground, I realised they were fighting, but not particularly well. They were taking potshots at each other, but it all seemed to be happening in slow motion and instead of landing punches, they were wrestling each other almost half-heartedly.

The white rabbit stood to the side, watching them.

"Halt! Police!" I shouted. To be sure, I was no longer the police, but I'd always found this an effective way of breaking up fist fights.

It worked like a charm this time, too.

The pair pulled apart and turned as one to stare at me. A large rotund woman wearing a nightshirt, curlers in her peroxide hair, and an equally round man, a little shorter than the woman, with a bald head and fully dressed in outdoor clothes.

"Polis?" he asked.

"What's going on?" I demanded. "Why are you fighting in the street? Don't you know that's a public order offence?"

The man wobbled and pointed a thick finger at the woman. "She started it." His words were slurred, his eyes glassy. I could only hazard a guess that he'd had a few too many beers.

The woman turned on him, her face contorted with rage. "Whaddayamean?" She swung for him, and as her big soft fist made contact, his poor balance caused them both to fall sideways into the nearest doorway in a heap. It might have been comical, but for the time being I could only feel annoyed.

I stepped forward to give them a hand up. They didn't seem dangerous, just irritating. But the woman had begun to squeal and was frantically pushing the man away from her.

"Calm down, calm down," he kept repeating.

"Let me up!" she shrieked. "Let me up!"

The white rabbit hopped nonchalantly away, towards the graffitied wall that bricked off Packhorse Close and prevented thoroughfare, then paused to observe the shenanigans.

The woman shrieked again, sounding increasingly panicked. I reached down to haul the man away from the woman, but he was a ton weight and I wasn't strong enough. All I could do was steady him as he slowly and painfully pulled himself upright. I pushed him out of the way and stepped in to help the woman to her feet as well, but I didn't need to. As soon as the man had climbed off her, she jumped up like a jack-in-the-box and backed away, wagging a finger at the doorway.

I illuminated the tip of my wand and gazed down at

what I instantly recognised as another body, covered in a sleeping bag rather than tucked inside it.

Just like the ones before.

"He did it!" The woman told me, pointing at the round man. "It was him!"

"You're a liar!" he shouted back at her. "I saw you here, leaning over him!"

"I was checking he was alright!"

"You were robbing him blind!"

"Well, what if I was? You wanted a share of it!"

"Hey!" I bellowed. "That's enough." I gestured with my wand at the doorway to the right. "One of you get in there and put your hands against the wall. The other …" I glanced around. The white rabbit stared solemnly at me, his back to the parameter wall. "Huh … in the next one."

The man blinked slowly but did as I said, slapping his doughy palms against the brickwork of the doorway. "Bind," I said, and a thin blue cord of ribbon erupted from my wand and bound the man's hands together, like a pair of handcuffs. But better because you couldn't lose the key.

The woman stared at me reproachfully, tears in her eyes. "Are you arresting us?" she asked.

"Of course I am," I said. When she didn't immediately move, I sent a frisson of sharp energy her way, giving her a small electric shock. That made her mind up. Bottom lip wobbling, she slunk into the next doorway. "Bind!" I snapped, and the cord made short work of securing her.

She wailed in deep anguish.

I knelt beside the body and reached towards the neckline. I could tell by the temperature of the skin it wouldn't be good news. I searched in vain for a pulse.

"Is he dead?" the man asked, looking over at me, his eyes full of fear.

"Very," I replied, securing my wand and reaching inside my bag for my phone. As I waited for the call to Monkton to connect, I surveyed my surroundings. Unless I was very much mistaken, this doorway was exactly the same one in which I'd found the previous body.

There was no way this was a coincidence.

I glanced up, seeking the rabbit. He'd disappeared. It might have been my imagination, but the wall at the end of the close seemed to shimmer.

I stood up and walked the thirty or so feet in that direction.

Monkton answered the phone with a growl. "It's late, Liddell. DCI Wyld is leaving the building."

"You'd better head this way, then." I lay my hand against the wall. Old red brick, like so much of Tumble Town. The pointing was beginning to wear away, but it was solid enough. "I've found another body."

"Ohhhhhh." Monkton's groan was heartfelt. "Where?"

"Exactly the same place as last time."

"I don't believe you."

"Believe it," I said, wondering where the white rabbit had disappeared to. I couldn't see an obvious rabbit-sized hole, but I suppose rabbits are small enough to get through quite tiny spaces.

"The same MO as before?"

I glanced back at the sleeping bag-covered lump that had once been someone's son. "I think so." The woman in the doorway was still whining.

"This time, I may have a suspect for you."

"Hallelujah! Sit tight, Liddell. I'm on my way."

I hung up and walked slowly back to the body. Normally I wouldn't have touched it but, right now, there was something I needed to know. I knelt beside the man, relatively young—my age perhaps—and eased the sleeping bag away from his right arm. I gently turned his wrist so I could see the underside of his arm.

There was the tattoo. Just the same as the second victim.

A labyrinth.

Not for the first time, I was left to wonder what it could signify …

## CHAPTER 13

"You know you should really be my chief suspect," Monkton was saying. "It's all a bit weird you finding these bodies."

I stared at the brick wall ahead of us and decided not to mention the white rabbit again. Monkton sounded exasperated enough.

"And if that wasn't enough, two in the same place!"

I couldn't help but agree with him.

"What do you make of that pair?" Monkton asked me, indicating my two round friends who were being led away down Packhorse Close by a couple of uniformed officers.

"I don't make much of them at all, to be honest." I stifled a yawn. It was twenty past ten and my feet were killing me. Never mind a bath, I'd settle for a spit wash and the opportunity to dive under my covers before midnight. "Any chance I can go home now?"

"You don't like them for it?" Monkton, his own black

eye bags taking up a large proportion of his face, looked exactly how I felt. It had been a long day for both of us.

"No, I don't think so."

"He accused her," Monkton pointed out.

"He did," I nodded, "but he's a) drunk and b) not the full ticket, I reckon."

"You can't go around dismissing witness testimony on the grounds that said witness is—"

"As sharp as a bowling ball?"

"Elise—"

"Let's face it," I grumbled, "that man couldn't pour water out of a Wellington boot if the instructions were printed on the heel. Any jury would dismiss his testimony out of court, not on the grounds of his lack of an IQ, but just based on his level of inebriation alone. I've seen students at a free bar more sober than he is."

"But—"

"It's much more likely that what *she* said is true. She was rolling a drunk. Unfortunately, her drunk turned out to be a dead man rather than an old soak."

"Ugh." Monkton rubbed his eyes and I took pity on him.

I pulled out a packet of mints from my pocket and offered him one. "The sugar will do you good."

He examined the packet with evident distrust. "These are sugar free."

"A healthier alternative to a fake sugar rush," I suggested. "Do you have *any* suspects at all?"

"Not one."

"But Mickey showed you the tattoos, didn't he?"

119

Monkton glared at me. "How do you know about those?"

I shrugged. "Don't ask me to reveal my sources."

"You're not supposed to be investigating this!" Monkton hissed at me.

"What difference does it make? You need help. You're not exactly sucking on diesel here!"

Monkton glared at me. "You're a *private* investigator, and this is a *public* case."

"I'm taking a private interest." I squared up to my ex-boss. "This is personal. Makepeace—"

"His involvement in what happened with Pritchard was minimal."

"I don't know how you can say that!" I folded my arms, completely exasperated. "We have no idea exactly what went on between those two, and—"

"That's where you're wrong, ex-DI Smartypants!"

"What do you mean?"

"I mean, earlier today Cerys confessed to the murder of Wizard Elryn Dodo, proprietor of a business of the same name on the premises at 125C Tudor Lane, Tumble Town. We have a signed confession, Elise. That case is done and dusted."

I was taken aback. "Wow."

"Your visit really shook her up. She spent the rest of the afternoon and evening trying to destroy her cell before the warders had her tranquilised. According to them, she then huddled in the corner and rocked for twenty-four hours. This morning she indicated she wanted to make a statement." Monkton smirked in satisfaction.

"What did she say about Makepeace?" I asked.

"She didn't mention him."

"*At all?*" My incredulous voice echoed around the narrow confines of Packhorse Close, and several officers turned to look at me.

"Nope."

"Then she's not telling you the whole truth!"

"Whatever." Monkton waved his hand as though to disregard the concept of 'whole truth'. "How often do we ever get right to the bottom of a case?"

"Rarely. But—"

"We can never know everything that has gone on. Given the stats that I have to deliver to the Chief Constable every Monday morning, believe me when I say I'll settle for a confession and a potential"—he nodded knowingly at me—"note my meaning here, *a potential*, dead accomplice."

"Makepeace isn't potentially dead," I argued. "He's totally dead."

"You know what I mean. Potentially he was a suspect in the murder of Wizard Dodo, but now we have a confession."

I was starting to lose the will to live. Monkton could frustrate the stuffing out of me sometimes. "But that *potential* suspect is dead too. That's not a coincidence."

"It is within the realms of probability that it is, in fact, a coincidence," Monkton told me. "We're looking into the deaths—three of them now—of three young homeless men. If Makepeace was spooked by what Pritchard did, then he may have well have tried to hide out in Tumble Town."

I tried to hold my tongue, I promise I did, but it was something that I'd never been very good at. "I think you're wrong," I stated baldly. "And I'll prove it to you."

I pushed past Monkton and then past a pair of young MOWPD constables who were guarding access to the scene. One of them made a grab for me, but I shot a malicious glare his way and he rapidly backed off.

Mickey O'Mahoney was crouched over the latest body. "Hey, Mickey?" I shouted as Monkton clamped a cast-iron grip on my shoulder.

Mickey's head jerked up on hearing my voice.

"What's the cause of death?" I asked, knowing he wouldn't answer. Couldn't. Not with the DCI standing right behind me. I grabbed my own throat in a pretend death grip with my right hand and grimaced.

"You know I can't tell you that," Mickey answered, narrowing his eyes at me, but he rolled his head around on his shoulders and nodded once.

"What—?" Monkton let go of my shoulder. "What's he saying?"

I spun to face him. "I think if you take a fresh look at the evidence, you'll see that the injuries on Makepeace are different from these latter two bodies that I've conveniently located for you."

"Alright," Monkton said. "I can take a look. You need to stay out of this, though. It's not your case."

As if I was going to do that. "My theory is we're looking for two killers," I told him. "And the person who killed Makepeace is linked to my Wizard Dodo case. I'm not letting this go."

Before he could protest any further, I swung on my heel and marched away.

"Elise?" I heard him call after me. When I kept right on going, he shouted louder, "Hey? Liddell!"

But I didn't so much as glance back.

I didn't work for him anymore.

I could do what I liked.

What I liked, it turned out, was to be back at my desk by seven the next morning.

Ezra was slumbering in his chair, feet up; he barely paused in his snoring as I entered the office and made a beeline first for the radiator to check it was on, and secondly for the kettle. My hair was still wet from my shower this morning, and I needed to warm up.

"It's freezing in here," I grumbled as I switched my computer on. Even it took longer to warm up than normal.

I snatched a post-it off my screen. It reminded me to buy some new boots for Snitch—*Size 10* it read … for a small man he certainly had huge feet—and opened up the Wonderland Database Wootton had designed for us.

I was beginning to put a file together based on the information I had from the murder scene the night before—and there wasn't much—when the phone on Wootton's desk rang. I transferred the call to my own phone.

"Wonderland Detective Agency, Elise Liddell speaking."

There was a pause, then a snort. "Wonderland?"

I recognised the gruff sing-song Irish accent. "Mickey?"

"Aye." In the background I could hear vehicles lumbering past him.

"It sounds as though you're camped out on a roundabout," I said.

"I'm on my way home. I've just pulled an all-nighter."

"Oh, dear. You have my commiserations."

"For what that's worth." He sounded tired. "Listen. I shouldn't really be talking to you, but I may have something for you?"

"Oooh! Yes?" With a thrill of excitement, I reached for a pencil.

"The guy who was brought in last night? He'd been stripped of everything that might have identified him."

"Hmpf." That was no help.

"But I couldn't help overhearing your conversation with DCI Wyld—"

I cringed. "Yeah, sorry. He's a cranky, pompous—"

"Yeah yeah. You adore him." Mickey sounded amused. "But I don't want you to go off like a rocket in pursuit of something or someone that's probably a red herring."

I frowned into the receiver. "What do you mean?"

"There *are* similarities between the bodies in terms of injuries."

"The crushed throat?"

"There is that, for the second two at least, but also …"

"If you're talking about the tattoo, then sure, I already know about that."

"You know?" Mickey sounded annoyed.

"Yes." I thought quickly and decided it would be better to lie. If I admitted what Ezra had done, Mickey would never allow me anywhere near his lab again. "I noticed it at the crime scene and I've been looking out for it ever since."

"Interesting."

"I understand what you're saying. We can't discount the fact that Makepeace had exactly the same tattoo as the latest two victims ... but don't you agree that the means of death are different?"

Mickey sighed. "Ah come on, Elise. You know that a serial killer changes his modus operandi as he becomes more confident."

"I do know that—"

"So why not let Wyld get on with his job?"

*No.* "Have you managed to find out how Makepeace died yet?"

"Nothing conclusive."

"Would you let me know when you do find something out?"

"No."

"I appreciate it," I smiled.

"Absolutely not."

"Call me when you have something," I told him.

"I definitely won't."

"Goodnight, sweet dreams!"

He hung up.

I smirked, knowing I'd get around him somehow,

and downed tools in preference of making myself a coffee. The kettle had boiled but cooled off, so I waited beside it this time, ready to fill the cafetière.

"Morning, boss!" Wootton stomped into the kitchen.

"You're early," I said and waved the coffee pot at him.

He nodded happily. "Please. Yeah." He unwound a colourful scarf from around his neck. "It's a cold one this morning. I've been awake half the night thinking about Culpeper."

"Did you come to any conclusions?" I asked hopefully.

"None."

"It's perfectly feasible that the records simply don't exist," I reminded him.

"But it's worth double-checking," he said. Wootton was nothing, if not thorough. "Why are you here so early? Does it have anything to do with the body found over in Packhorse Close last night?" He smiled slyly.

"Good news travels fast."

"Bad news travels faster than wildfire," Wootton nodded. "I bumped into Snitch. He was hanging around trying to talk to Shadow People, I think."

Someone else who hadn't had much sleep. It seemed like Ezra, who needed it the least, had enjoyed the best night of us all.

I poured coffee for us both and handed his mug over.

"I'd best get started," he said.

"Before you do," I said, leading him back into the office so that Ezra could hear, "I want us to take a closer look at Packhorse Close."

"Because that's where the last two murders were, right?" Wootton asked.

"Yes. I can't help feeling that Makepeace is the odd one out. Which makes me think that including him in this batch of murders is simply clouding DCI Wyld's thinking."

"Are you going back over there to have another look at the scene?"

I could tell by the glint in Wootton's eyes that he wanted to come with me. "A little later," I said, "and no, you can't come."

"I'm sure a dead-end lane won't be even remotely dangerous," he said. "It would be awesome to get a little field experience."

"You're my administrator," I reminded him. "Stick to administrator-ing."

Wootton grunted. "With a vocabulary like that, it's no wonder you need someone to type up all your reports."

I winked at Ezra. He hid a smile.

"Get that computer of yours up and running," I said. "I need information."

"Packhorse Close *and* Culpeper?" he checked. To give him credit where it was due, Wootton didn't remain sullen for long.

"Yes please."

"You've got it, Grandma."

≈

"Well …" Wootton swung his chair back. Not for the first time, I made a mental note to buy him a proper office chair with wheels. It would be cheaper than being sued when he fell backwards out of the window and landed in a crumpled broken heap in front of The Hat and Dashery.

"Do you have something?" Ezra asked.

"I think I do." Wootton frowned at his screen. I rose from my desk where I'd been scanning missing persons' reports in the National Police Database and squeezed in behind his desk to take a look.

"See here?" Wootton ran his finger across his screen as Ezra joined us. He'd been searching the newspaper archive again. In this case, he was looking at a report from *The Celestine Times*. "This is dated the eighteenth of October 2004."

"A murder?" I scanned the article.

"In Packhorse Close no less. An unidentified man in his twenties."

"Could be a coincidence," Ezra shrugged. "This is Tumble Town, after all."

"Could be," I agreed. It was always better to keep an open mind about these things. "Any mention of a tattoo or how he died?" I asked.

"No," Wootton said. "And in fact, apart from a mention the following week, there were no other updates."

"Nobody was interested?" It shouldn't have surprised me. I'd worked on so many murder cases over the years, but by far the saddest were the ones where nobody seemed to care one way or the other. I supposed that was par for the course where the homeless and destitute were concerned.

"Apparently not."

"Perhaps Mickey could get me the records relating to that case," I wondered aloud. "I know it was before his time, but he would be able to check it out."

"He might thank you for the information," Ezra agreed. "It's likely he doesn't know about it either."

I nodded. "I'll give Mickey a shout. Oh, and I'll call Monkton too. I think this is information we should share. I don't want him to accuse us of stomping all over his case."

"That's not all though." Wootton flicked to another screen. "There was another one in 1994. Again. Just a cursory report and then no follow-up."

"That's really odd." Ezra met my eyes, nodding slowly. "Too much of a coincidence."

"I agree." I made my way over to my desk. "Send me the links for those articles, Wootton. Let me have a closer look at them."

"Will do. I'll research further back too."

"Good idea." I plucked up the post-it from my desk, the one reminding me I needed to go shopping. "While you do that, I just want to nip out. I won't be long."

"Hmm. We've heard that one before." Wootton rolled his eyes. "You nipping out invariably leads to the discovery of another murder, or you go AWOL for hours."

"I swear this time, I'll be back soon."

"Alright. Is it your turn to buy the office elevenses, by any chance?" Wootton asked hopefully.

"I'll add cakes to the list," I said, grabbing my bag.

Of course, by the time I'd chatted with Hattie about the best place to buy good solid walking boots for Snitch then walked over there and perused the selection, bought some, and then walked back via Betty's and queued up and chosen cakes for me, Wootton, Hattie and Snitch, then returned to see Hattie to hand over her cake and show her the boots—well, more time had passed than I'd intended.

Never mind elevenses, we'd have to consume our sweet treats over lunch instead.

"Hello!" I called as I clumped up the stairs, but the only person inhabiting the office was Ezra. "Are you on your own?" I checked the time. Just before midday. Wootton didn't normally take his lunch break till one-ish.

Ezra regarded me with surprise. "Didn't Wootton find you?"

"Find me?"

"He was all excited by something he unearthed on his computer. He tried to call you, but you left your mobile on the desk."

"I did. So ... what?" I attempted to quash a little niggle of apprehension fluttering in my chest. "He came after me to the shoe shop or ...?"

"You've been shopping?"

The niggle grew and began to frizz with alarm. "Where did Wootton think I was going?"

"To Packhorse Close."

"And you let him go alone?" I dumped my shopping on the floor and picked up my phone, as though that would somehow alert me to what Wootton had wanted to tell me that was so important he couldn't wait for me to return.

"You're not thinking something bad will happen to him, surely?" Ezra asked.

"I'm not sure what I'm thinking." I quickly put a call through to Wootton's mobile. It went directly to voicemail. I pocketed my phone and checked I had my wand. "I should go after him."

"I'm sure he'll be fine," Ezra said, but even he looked concerned.

"I know. I'm probably overreacting," I admitted. "I just have an increasingly bad feeling about that place." I moved over to Wootton's desk to glance at the notes by the side of his computer. There was a list of dates jotted down: *1998. 1992. 1987. 1979. 1967. 1954.*

And more.

Could these all be related to Packhorse Close?

More murders?

I wiggled Wootton's computer mouse to wake up his machine and flicked through his windows. Definitely more murders. I scanned the headlines of newspaper reports he had saved.

*An Unfortunate Incident.*

*Tragic Case of Itinerant Worker.*

*Down and Out Perishes in Snowstorm.*

"What is going on here? This is looking increasingly messy." I shivered. "I need to find Wootton."

"I'll come with you." Ezra floated upright.

"No. It would be better if you stay here, we can't leave the office unmanned. But if Snitch turns up, send him along to meet me."

"Will do." Ezra nodded. I turned to leave. "And Elise?"

I glanced back.

"Stop worrying. I'm sure it will all be fine." I spotted the unease in his own eyes. He had always trusted my sixth sense. Right now, that was clanging like the bells of Big Ben.

"I hope you're right."

# CHAPTER 14

Packhorse Close looked different during the day. I'd been here before, but this time I made every effort to really try and view it objectively. I walked the length of the narrow lane slowly, taking in the run-down houses, the solidity of the brick buildings, the crumbling plaster, the flaking paintwork. Several houses closest to the junction with Cross Lane had been modernised. One or two even had double glazing, but the vast majority on both sides still had their original sash windows. I could imagine the sound of glass panes rattling on a windy day.

Closer to the wall at the opposite end of the close, the houses were in the worst state. More run-down than their neighbours, graffiti scrawled across the external walls, the doors replaced by heavy barriers with the occasional 'Keep Out' sign, hazard signs, or warnings against trespassers.

Blue and white tape fluttered around the doorway where both of the recent bodies had been discovered.

*Police Line – Do not cross*, it demanded, but it had been yanked away from the scene and now flapped freely in the breeze, forlorn in the quiet solitude of the deserted alleyway.

Of Wootton, there was no sign.

I rang the office to check that I hadn't missed his return. Ezra confirmed that he hadn't made it back so far. After agreeing that he would call me if he did, I hung up and began another circuit of Packhorse Close.

The police had swept the alley clean while searching for evidence, but already piles of rubbish were beginning to mount up. I walked backwards and forwards, separating bundles of paper and cans with my booted foot, occasionally rummaging through what I found. But there was nothing of interest.

The second time I reached the wall, I stood and studied it for the longest time. Graffiti artists had daubed the wall over and over again, so the original brickwork could hardly be seen. Layers and layers of paint obscured older designs. In the daylight, it just looked like a mess. I imagined that if I had a more contemporary artistic bent or an understanding of urban culture, I might appreciate the designs more.

Maybe.

Remembering how the wall had seemed to shimmer the night before, I ran my fingers across the surface, tracing the shallow dips between the bricks. It all seemed solid enough to me.

"It's an eyesore, isn't it?"

A gruff voice interrupted my thoughts. I glanced sideways and then down. A small but thick-set man, not quite four feet tall, stared up at me with bright eyes. I couldn't tell how old he was, but I would have hazarded a guess at somewhere in his sixties. The yellowy-green tinge to his tanned skin suggested he was at least part goblin. The dark green of his long robes and the twisted staff he carried told me he was a wizard.

"It's not pretty," I admitted. "I wonder why they thought they would build it here?"

The wizard regarded me, his face solemn, but he didn't venture an opinion.

"What's on the other side?" I asked. "Any idea?"

He shrugged. "The other half of Packhorse Way, I should imagine."

"Packhorse Way?" I asked. "I thought this was Packhorse Close?"

"They renamed it when they built the wall."

He certainly seemed to know a lot about it. "Do you live near here?" I asked, looking around. I hadn't seen where he'd come from.

He pointed back at a door that had been painted the same colour green as his robes. The last habitable house on that side and only two doors down from the doorway of death, as I'd come to think of it.

"I was looking for my friend," I told him. "A young man, early twenties."

"Silly hair?" the goblin wizard asked, and I nodded. It wasn't that Wootton had silly hair as such, but it was perhaps a more modern style than the goblin would appreciate.

"No," he said and began to hobble back towards his house. "Haven't seen him."

His response was so absurd that I laughed in spite of myself.

The goblin stopped and looked back at me. "I amuse you, do I?"

"I'm sorry," I said, getting myself under control. "It's just I'm really concerned for his welfare, and it seemed as though you had seen someone who fitted his description."

"I asked you if he had silly hair. Too many people have silly hair these days." He gestured towards my head with his staff.

*Touché.*

"How long have you lived here?" I asked.

"Always," he said, and resumed his path towards his front door. I followed him, a little tentatively. I didn't want to be on the receiving end of the knuckled knob of his staff. When he reached his doorstep, swept clean I noted, he paused and looked back at me. "Are you the police?" he asked.

I decided he'd probably see through a lie, so I played it straight. "I used to be. Now I'm a private investigator. I have my own detective agency in Tudor Lane." I fished in my pocket for my card and edged closer so I could offer it to him.

He took it and flipped it over, squinting at the small lettering. "Wonderland Detective Agency?"

"That's right. The young man I'm looking for—he's called Wootton—works for me."

"So, you're not investigating the murders, then?"

I met his eyes. I could see the keen intelligence burning there. From his front window, he would have been able to see a lot that went on in the immediate vicinity of his house. I had a feeling he knew more than he was letting on.

In fact, if he'd been paying attention recently, he would have seen me here on more than one occasion.

There didn't seem any point in telling porky pies.

"I was the one who discovered the bodies." I thought about the list on Wootton's desk with all the dates on. "The last two, at any rate. I can't lie, I'm intrigued, but it's not my case as such."

"I see." He looked me up and down, from my rainbow-coloured hair to the mucky boots on my feet. "You'd best come in. But please wipe your feet. Better still, take those great clod-hopping shoes off." He unlocked his door and pushed it open. "Leave them in the hallway, not on the step. You'd never see them again otherwise."

I did as he asked. He waited for me to sort myself out then showed me into the small front room—it might have been called the parlour once upon a time—where a cosy fire burned brightly and the sweet scent of pipe tobacco made me nostalgic for my grandfather.

On either side of the fireplace, shelves had been set into the wall. A variety of books lined them, most of them literature rather than books about magick, and an array of photographs neatly arranged in frames. The wizard goblin when he was a young man and various family members, I guessed.

"I hope you like Goblin Gunpowder tea? It's all I ever drink, but it might be a little strong for your taste."

"I like strong tea," I told him. "I hope I'm not putting

you to any bother, Wizard—?" I raised my eyes expectantly.

After a beat, he grudgingly gave up his name. "Wizard Gambol. Glyrk Gambol. And yes." He curled a lip at me, but not in a fierce way. "You most decidedly *are* putting me out."

Before I could respond, he disappeared out into the hallway again, and a moment or so later I heard the clang of something metallic and the clink of crockery as he prepared his tea. He hadn't asked me to sit, and although I might have guessed to take the two-seater sofa on the grounds that his preference would be for the only armchair, I didn't like to be presumptuous. I wandered to the window and moved the thick nets aside so I could peer out into Pack-horse Close. I could clearly see the wall to my left, and if I turned my head and squished my ear against the glass, I could see the doorway of death to my right.

Behind me, the wizard cleared his throat. Guiltily, I returned my attention to him. He placed the tray on a small table and centred it between his armchair and the sofa.

"Please," he said, and I came to sit opposite him. We lapsed into silence.

"It's a lovely place you have here," I said eventually, by way of conversation rather than anything else.

"It's a home," Gambol agreed.

"Warm and cosy." I couldn't help myself; I glanced towards the window.

"With a good view of the comings and goings,"

Gambol said, and I thought I heard a certain invitation in his tone.

"The police must have interviewed you."

"I have no dealings with that lot," Gambol said. "Not many in Tumble Town do." He regarded me with those bright, inquisitive eyes of his. "You've crossed the tracks. Changed sides—"

"I live and work here now, yes," I said. "I'm not sure I've changed—"

"Give it time," Gambol cut me off. "Eventually, we all switch allegiances."

I opened my mouth to protest, then closed it again. He was entitled to his opinion, however misplaced that might have been. I didn't want to upset him.

He poured the tea and handed me a clumsy pottery beaker. I didn't even need to take a sip to recognise how strong the liquid would be. I could smell it. It made my eyes water.

"There's milk and sugar there if you want to ruin a perfectly decent cuppa," Gambol said, and I gratefully made a dive for both, ignoring his grumpy glare.

"I really should be out there looking for my friend," I fretted.

"Chances are either he's alright or he isn't," Wizard Gambol said helpfully.

"What if he isn't?" I asked. "What's if he's somewhere between those two states?"

"Then you would need to find him urgently."

Something twisted in my stomach and I jumped up. I shouldn't be in this little house playing word games with a wizard goblin. Wootton might be in danger.

Look what had happened to Ezra. I couldn't coun-
tenance—

"Such panic." The wizard shook his head.

I glanced out of the window and Gambol followed
my gaze. "You should probably go after him," he said
slowly, "but forewarned is forearmed."

"Go after him? Go where?"

Gambol reluctantly pushed himself from his comfy
seat and came to stand by me. We stared out of the
window together. He pointed in the direction of the
wall. "It's a rabbit hole."

I frowned. "There's a rabbit hole there? I've been
seeing a rabbit, but I doubt Wootton would fit in a
rabbit's burrow. I mean, he's slim but he's not that lithe."

"A rabbit hole," Wizard Gambol repeated. "Like a
black hole. Or a wormhole."

I was still none the wiser.

He wheezed out a deep sigh. "Like a portal?" He
arched an eyebrow.

My jaw dropped. I hadn't given that any considera-
tion at all. Tumble Town, I'd been reliably informed,
was a warren—excuse the pun—of portals in places
where you wouldn't expect to find them. But that was
the thing. Unless you actively went looking for them, or
knew they were there, then you were unlikely to
stumble upon one by accident.

"The wall—?"

"Was built to block it. But magick being magick, it
sometimes doesn't work." He shrugged and retreated to
his armchair, clambering up and rescuing his tea, his
little legs dangling a foot above the floor.

I followed him, perching on the edge of the sofa. "Can you explain?" I asked him. "Do you think Wootton might have gone through it somehow? Can I get him back?"

"So many questions." Wizard Gambol twinkled at me and I realised he was enjoying himself now. A typical goblin, thriving on someone else's misfortune. "You should answer a few questions for me first. A kind of exchange of information, if you like."

"An exchange of information," I repeated, unsure I liked the sound of that.

He sensed my reluctance. "Otherwise, how can I know you're trustworthy?"

I gave him a little dead-eye. This was entirely part of his process; I could see that. "What do you want to know?"

He rubbed his palms together. "You said you've been seeing a rabbit?"

I nodded.

"What colour?"

"White."

"Red eyes?"

"No. Brown eyes."

"Ooooooh." He sipped his tea, thinking. "Intriguing."

"Is it?"

He considered me, the sides of his mouth curling. There was something not entirely pleasant about his expression.

"It's not usually a white rabbit."

"Pardon me?"

"When people receive an invitation, it's not usually a

white rabbit," Gambol repeated, his tone a little delicate as though he were sharing a secret.

"The white rabbit is an invitation?" The thought astonished me. Truth to tell though, there had been something unusual about it.

"It is."

"Let me get this straight," I said. "You're suggesting I have an invitation to follow the white rabbit into the 'rabbit hole'?"

"That's about the shape of it." He emitted a high-pitched giggle.

I regarded him with some trepidation. It seemed a little out of character for him.

"You might have noticed if you hadn't allowed your-self to be side-tracked by dead men in doorways," he growled.

The change in his tone unnerved me. A little alarm bell began to clang in the corner of my head. It kept time with the frisson of anxiety that pulsed through my body whenever I thought about Wootton.

"Are you going to tell me what you know about the murders?" I challenged him.

"Certainly not," Gambol hissed. "I told you. I have no dealings with the police."

"That's not very helpful."

"It's not my job to help you people."

"What is your job?"

He leered at me, but remained silent.

"What's through the rabbit hole?" I tried to engage him again.

"You should search for a way in. Go through. Then you'll find out, won't you?"

"Have you been through?"

He shook his head. "No, no, no. Not me. I told you, you need an invitation. I've never received one."

The rabbit, he meant.

"Is the colour of the rabbit important?" I asked.

Gambol was quiet, avoiding making eye contact as he refilled his beaker with the increasingly stewed blend of tea. The stink of it was making me nauseous. Beside me, the fire crackled. The heat from it made my eyes smart.

Eventually, when I thought I couldn't stand the stultifying oppression of the room any longer, he looked up. "Those in the know would say that the colour of the rabbit is symbolic. Brown rabbits are supposedly sent out to seek new recruits."

"Recruits for what?"

Gambol ignored the question. "Black rabbits mean death."

I shuddered, only pleased that I hadn't seen a black rabbit. "So, what about white rabbits then? They're 'invitations'? To what?"

Now even Wizard Gambol seemed perplexed. "I've never seen one myself, you understand, but I've heard that a white rabbit with red eyes signifies treachery."

"My rabbit doesn't have red eyes," I reminded him. "They were definitely brown. A beautiful brown. Like melted chocolate."

Gambol curled his lip. "I have no idea. You'll have to take your chances."

"Take my chances? I really don't like the sound of that."

A shadow temporarily blocked the light and I glanced at the window. Someone had walked along the alley, heading towards the wall end of Packhorse Close. I jumped up. Had that been Snitch?

Wizard Gambol remained in his chair. "What choice do you have? The rabbit hole is calling you. It is your fate."

CHAPTER 15

"Give me a moment, please!" I placed my beaker of extraordinarily strong tea on the coffee table and made a dash into the hall-way. I hastily tugged my boots on, leaving them unlaced, and yanked open the door.

Snitch was crouching next to the wall, his head tipped at an angle as he scrutinised something close to the ground.

"Snitch?" I called. "Snitch!"

He stood up and dusted off his robes. "Hey, Elise. Ezra told me to come and find you." He pointed down at the foot of the wall. "The strangest thing just happened."

"What?" I asked, not feeling entirely easy about the light shining in Snitch's eyes.

"I followed a rabbit all the way from Cross Lane to this point. It was almost like it knew I was coming here."

"What colour was it?" I asked.

"Brown. Rabbit coloured."

My stomach twisted. "Not all rabbits are brown, Snitch. The one I've been seeing is white." Assuming it was the same one every time it showed up, of course.

"What a thing, eh? I never knew there were so many rabbits in Tumble Town." Snitch's face was a picture.

I hated to burst his bubble. "I really don't think they're native to the area."

"It disappeared behind the wall here," he pointed. "Through that hole."

"What hole?" I couldn't see a hole.

"There!" Snitch sounded frustrated by my stupidity. He gestured with his foot. "I could just about wriggle through—" He crouched down again.

I yanked his arm and pulled him up again. "No!"

"What's the matter? I just want to see where the bunny went!"

I grabbed his shoulders. I needed him to pay attention. "It's not a cute flipsy-flopsy bunny wunny though. That's the problem!"

"What—?"

"Somehow, these rabbits are linked to the deaths of men in Packhorse Close. Not just the two men I've found but others. Wootton did some research, and bodies have been turning up here sporadically for decades. If not longer." I pointed in the direction of Wizard Gambol's house. "I've just been informed that—"

I stopped.

And blinked.

What had been Wizard Gambol's warm and cheerful dwelling with its green paint that matched his robes and heavy nets at the window was now a dilapidated and run-down hovel.

I caught my breath and released Snitch from my tight gasp, stumbling up the close. Maybe I was looking for the door in the wrong place. But no. None of the doors around me were green.

I rubbed my forehead.

"I never heard of a rabbit committing murder." From behind me, Snitch sounded dubious. "It was weird how it seemed to lead me here and disappear down the hole—"

I whirled around. "Show me the hole," I demanded.

Snitch shot me a wary look. "It's just there, Elise."

"I can't see a hole! Put your hand in it! Show me exactly where it is."

"It's right here." Snitch knelt down again. "Right in the centre of the target."

"Target? I don't see a target either."

I watched as Snitch's hand seemed to disappear into the brickwork. "Whoa." I crouched down beside him and reached for the place where his hand should have been, but I skinned my knuckles on the wall above him.

"Ow!" I withdrew my hand and showed him the sudden bloom of blood on my middle finger, the scraped skin on the fingers on either side. "There is no hole there for me."

Snitch paled and hurriedly pulled his own hand out of the hole. We stood together and slowly backed away, Snitch running his tongue over his bottom lip. "Huh."

"Describe what you see when you look at the wall," I asked him.

"You think we're seeing different things, don't you?" Snitch swallowed hard. I nodded. "Right, well … I see circles. Blue and white." He gestured up at the centre of the wall and then allowed his left hand to drift further left. "And a kind of chequered pattern around the outside of those and … a big off-centre target." He dropped his right hand towards the bottom right of the wall where his hole had been. "In red."

"You can see a target?" He'd mentioned that before.

"It looks kind of like a slightly skew-whiff mod design. Like you'd see on a scooter or something. I like it. It reminds me of my youth."

"You like that kind of music?"

"Love it!" he enthused. "What do you see?"

"I just see a mess of colourful graffiti. Big swirls of bright colour, and writing that makes no sense. You see red, white, blue and black, and I see purple, green, orange and yellow. Big fluorescent splashes of colour."

Snitch grimaced. "Sounds like some kind of neon hell."

"I like colour." I pointed at my hair and plucked a loop to show him. "Particularly this violet colour." I scrutinised the wall. "Which I can see here and here and here …"

"Maybe that's why you see graffiti and I see a target," he said, echoing my own thoughts. "We see what we like."

"But why don't I see a hole?"

"I definitely do. You know—" Snitch laughed, a hollow sound, then pulled a face. "I could go through? Report back?" He cast a doubtful glance at me.

"Absolutely not!" I grabbed his shoulder and dragged him further away. "We're going back to the office. Perhaps Wootton has checked in."

"He hadn't when I was there."

Increasingly, that's what I was afraid of. I reached into my pocket for my phone, thumbed the screen and held it up. Quickly I snapped a couple of photos of the wall.

"Let's get out of here," I said. "This place has started giving me the heebie-jeebies."

CHAPTER 16

"We now have a list of names from the National Missing Persons' Database. Ah, let me see ... DC Mires? If you and Quinn can run with those, see if any could potentially belong to either of our John Does, I'd be grateful—"

I popped my head around the door of the office I had once shared with Ezra and over a dozen ex-colleagues. It was nine in the morning, sunny outside, but you would never have known it. The homicide team had long ago been hidden away in the basement of the Ministry of Witches building, which seemed particularly fitting, given the type of cases they were dealing with. Certainly, this could be a dark, miserable space thanks to the lack of windows. To counteract this, bright lights had been strategically placed—although to be honest, given the amount of electronic equipment spread over the desks and workstations, and the screens that graced the walls, you tended not to notice there wasn't any natural light. Besides, only on rare occasions had I ever had to spend the whole day in the office. Most of my work had involved travelling around to different crime scenes or to all corners of the British Isles to interview suspects.

DCI Monkton Wyld was leaning against the wall with his hands folded over his chest, looking decidedly glum as he listened to DI Sal Roberto dish out tasks. My movement caught his eye. He looked around the room, then decided I could only be here for him, and abandoned his post.

"How did you get in here?" he hissed as he joined me at the door. A couple of the other officers turned their heads to look my way, so I bobbed out of view, stepping back into the safety of the corridor.

"The people at reception know me," I reminded him.

"Well, they should also know not to let you in," he grumbled. "I'll send a memo out to that effect."

"You do that." I glared back at him. "I would have thought you had more important things to do at the moment, though. How are your murder *cases* coming along?"

"Have you come here about those? You know I can't—"

"Yeah, yeah." I bit down on my sudden spark of fury. "You can't tell me anything. It's becoming monotonous. But don't worry, it's fine."

"I'm glad we're on the same page." Monkton gestured politely back towards the stairwell, insinuating now would be a good time to leave.

"But that's not why I'm here." I stubbornly held my ground. "I mean, not really. But it kind of is."

Monkton raised his shoulders to his ears in exasperation. "Is it, or isn't it?"

I came right out with it. "Wootton has disappeared."

"Wootton being—?"

"Wootton Fitzpaine," I reminded him. "You've met him several times. My office assistant."

"Ah, that's right. The young man." Monkton's face changed. Now he genuinely appeared concerned. "When was the last time you saw him?"

"Yesterday. At approximately nine in the morning. Quarter past. Maybe a little later. I was distracted." I breathed heavily. "I wanted to report this earlier but I knew I had better wait for at least twenty-four hours before coming to you."

"Go on." At least Monkton hadn't dismissed me out of hand.

"He was doing some research into Packhorse Close for me—"

"Hmmm?" Monkton rolled his eyes.

I ignored him. "I popped out and I was a little later back than I intended. We're not entirely sure where he went, but Ezra thinks he came after me, thinking I was going to Packhorse Close. Except I didn't. Not at that stage."

"Okay." Monkton looked a little bewildered. "Stupid question, but you've been attempting to call him?"

"Every fifteen minutes. I've checked his flat. I've checked with the landlord at The Pig and Pepper. Snitch has tried to find his friends. I've retraced his steps out of the office, and Snitch and Ezra have been asking around. But there's no sign of him. No sightings. Nothing."

"That's Tumble Town for you. Maybe he's with a girlfriend? Or a boyfriend? Or whatever his particular proclivity is?" Monkton raised his eyebrows in enquiry.

I shrugged. "If he's in a relationship, he's been keeping quiet about it. But besides that, there's no way he'd leave the office during the day and not come back. He would *always* keep me in the loop with what he's doing. He's incredibly focused. He goes on about how he wants to be a detective." The thought of that and what it might mean jabbed me hard in the ribs. "Monkton, I'm scared he followed me. What happens if he's the next victim? We have to find him."

Monkton held my gaze, his lips pressed firmly together while he thought. Finally, he wiggled his head. "Alright. Let's grab a coffee and you can tell me all."

We caught up over paper cups of dark coffee in the cafeteria. The bitterness of my drink reminded me of the Goblin Gunpowder tea, and I relayed that information to Monkton as well. At first, he simply sat opposite and listened, but eventually he reached for his notebook and jotted a few of the details down.

"I'd search those derelict properties at the bottom end of Packhorse Close," I said and swallowed hard. Please don't let Wootton be in there. Not hidden away beneath an old sleeping bag like a pile of cast-off rubbish.

He nodded. "I had our team check around those dwellings, but everything seemed secure and we didn't force entry. I'll look into that some more. We have cause to do so anyway." He tapped his nose with his pen. "What about this wizard and his rabbit story? What do you make of that?"

I blew my cheeks out. "Who knows? Really. I spent most of last night sitting in the office, waiting for Wootton to get in touch, thinking, thinking, thinking. I even went back to Packhorse Close and had another look, but I don't see what Snitch sees. There's no hole there for me."

"Maybe you should have let him go through it."

"Monkton!" I was appalled he would even consider such a thing.

Monkton lifted his hands in surrender. "Alright. I get why you didn't." He didn't sound as though he would have made the same decision as me, though.

I pulled out my mobile and showed him the photos I'd taken of the wall the previous day.

"They're blank," he said.

"That's right. When I went back to the office, I tried to upload them to my computer, but there was nothing to upload. As you can see"—I flicked through the images that came after—"there's nothing wrong with my phone, as battered as it is. The camera still works. There's something very odd about that wall."

"Could be a coincidence."

"Yes, but there are far too many coincidences where this mess is concerned."

He couldn't deny that. I let him flick through the images; it gave me time to think.

Eventually I asked, "What did that wall look like to you when you were in the alley?"

"I can't say I paid too much attention to it," he answered, "but yes, now I think about it, there was a funky old piano design that I liked."

"Funky old piano," I repeated. There was no funky old piano on 'my' wall.

"Mmm. Like an old jazz blues-type plinkity-plonk piano."

*Interesting.* Monkton loved jazz. Knowing him, plinkity-plonk was his favourite kind of sound. "That confirms this idea Snitch had, that we see what appeals to us."

"Is Snitch a detective-in-training too?" Monkton sneered.

"No." I gave my old boss a bit of frozen-eye. "He's just helping me out. Which is more than you're doing."

Monkton drained his coffee. "You know the MOWPD isn't supposed to get involved in situations across the way. Tumble Town has its own squad—"

"Who nobody ever sees!"

"Because that's the way they want it. I can't do anything about that." He sighed. "Look, I'll circulate a description of Wootton. Get everyone to look out for him. I can also ask my boss about putting a trace on his phone and his bank transactions. That'll alert us to him if he's moving around."

I didn't want to think about him not moving around. Not using his phone. Not spending any money.

Monkton drained his coffee and pushed himself to his feet. "I'd better be getting back to it. It's all a bit grim here today. We already have a 'missing persons' of sorts on the go this morning."

"Linked to Packhorse Close?" I asked.

"Yes." He shrugged. "It's probably something and nothing, but that pair you had us pick up when you found your third body? They've gone."

The drunk man and the round woman? "Missing?" I couldn't believe what I was hearing.

"Weird one. One of my officers went to interview them again last night, and it turns out that the address they gave us doesn't exist anymore. Or rather it does, but it's one of the derelict houses. That's why I want to take another look at those buildings."

"Do you think something's happened to them?"

"It seems more likely they've done a runner. Odd pair." He sniffed. "I'll put a team together to question the neighbours. Maybe they'll recognise them, maybe not. Maybe they'll tell us, maybe not." He shrugged. "Good job we managed to load their mugshots into the system. Perhaps I'll make a start with this wizard goblin friend of yours. What number does he live at?"

"I told you. The house was abandoned." Monkton clearly thought I'd dreamed the whole thing up. "But it was number sixty-seven. Good luck finding Gambol," I grumbled. "And if you do, tell him I want another word with him." I tailed off. I could see by the look on Monkton's face I'd hit a nerve. "What's up?"

"You said sixty-seven? Are you sure?"

"Yes. It had a green door." I rethought that. "Until it didn't, if you see what I mean."

"That's where Mr and Mrs Tweedle claimed to live."

"They were married?" That surprised me.

"That's what they said. I'm beginning to think they told us a number of untruths."

"No kidding."

"Yeah, 67 Packhorse Close. I'll double-check, but that's my recollection." He walked with me to the main entrance of the department. I waved at Berniece on reception. She winked back at me. "What are you intending to do now?" Monkton wanted to know.

"Maybe I'll head back down Packhorse Close and have another look at those buildings myself."

"Elise—"

"Don't worry. I won't be breaking and entering. It will all be within the limits of the law." Before he could protest any further, I reminded him of my primary focus. "I'm still searching for Wootton. I appreciate all you can do, but I need to be out there looking too!"

Monkton sucked in a breath. He couldn't stop me, and wouldn't. "Just be careful, okay? Keep me posted. Don't do anything or go anywhere that I wouldn't."

I patted his arm. "Don't worry."

The thing was, in all the years we'd worked together, Monkton had never been one for taking risks, whereas me?

I just couldn't help myself.

～

Monkton had been right about number 67 Packhorse Close.

The buildings were secure, at least at the front. The doors and windows were securely boarded up, and although I pushed and pulled at any point of access I thought might be weaker and allow me a glimpse inside the dwellings, I lucked out.

I banged harder on the door of number 67. "Wizard Gambol?" I called, but nobody answered.

The wind blew down the narrow alleyway. Dry leaves, dust, sweet wrappings and empty crisp bags danced around my feet. I meandered in the direction of Cross Lane, wondering whether to knock on a few doors myself, maybe ask whether anyone had seen Wootton until I spotted a couple of my ex-colleagues further up. They were going from door-to-door, and I could only assume they were making enquiries.

That was a load off my mind.

I waved when they glanced my way, just to let them know I was hanging around, and retreated further into the close to await their arrival at this end. The rubbish had started to pile up at the foot of the wall. It made little scratching sounds as it fought to carry on its journey but was thwarted in the attempt by the enormous barrier that blocked its path.

I knew how it felt.

I imagined the world with no such wall. How it *would have been* once upon a time. Before the days of plastic wrappings. When you would have been able to stroll down the length of Packhorse Way. Any rubbish—waxed paper in those days perhaps, or newspaper, certainly dead leaves—would have been able to emerge at the other side to continue its journey to who knew where. If I could get through, I'd be able to discover where the white rabbit lived. I'd be able—

The white rabbit!

It bobbed into view at the foot of the wall … in the exact same place where Snitch had claimed his hole was.

"Hey," I whispered, trying not to frighten it. I didn't really need to worry. I knew from experience that the little creature was as bold as brass.

It twitched its nose at me then retreated. I couldn't see where to. I moved directly to the place it had been and crouched down among the dust and the rubble, reaching out tentatively to move the bulkier bits of rubbish out of the way, scared of what horrors— meaning slimy insects and multi-legged creatures—I might find.

But actually, once I'd shifted a few soft drink bottles and a couple of old shopping bags, a number of cigarette butts and, more peculiarly, a doll's torso, what I found was a brick painted entirely white—apart from some small lettering.

I leaned closer to read what it said, imagining that, like most of the graffiti evident all over the wall, I wouldn't be able to understand it. I was wrong.

*Push me.*

"Push me?" I asked aloud, my voice sounding oddly breathy. "Push the brick?"

I didn't need to think twice. I reached out and pushed the brick.

## CHAPTER 17

At first, I thought I'd been taken for a mug. Nothing happened. My fingernails turned white as I pushed against the brick and all to no avail. I sat back on my haunches to consider my options, tapping the brick for good measure, but when I heard a faint click followed by a loud grinding noise, I shot backwards in alarm.

The ground beneath my feet vibrated. Within seconds, the whole world seemed to be shuddering.

*What have I done? Is this how an earthquake feels?*

A chink of light began to emanate from the centre of the wall. I moved further back to get a better—and safer —look at it. As I did so, the chink elongated and became a tall slither. The rumbling noise continued, and I realised that the wall had split in the middle and was opening away from me.

"Open sesame!" I said, marvelling at the scene.

I stretched my neck, angling my head to peer through the gap, curious about what I'd find on the other side, but the light was blinding, as though someone was directing a searchlight straight into my eyes. I couldn't see a thing.

Shielding my eyes against the glare, I stepped through the opening, forgetting about Monkton's police officers and only praying that the wall wouldn't suddenly close while I was making my way to the other side and thereby crush me to death.

I needn't have worried.

As I walked into the light, the rabbit appeared at my feet. It was the closest it had ever ventured to me. When I bent down to it, it allowed me to stroke its soft head for a moment before bouncing off sideways.

Uncertain of what I should be doing, and completely blind in any case, I followed it. The grinding noise came again, the ground shuddering beneath my feet. I whirled about as the wall slowly closed. If I had wanted to, I could have darted back to the 'right' side, but I had a feeling this was an opportunity I couldn't let slip.

With a terrific grating sound, the wall completely closed up. I couldn't get back now—not this way in any case—even if I wanted to. The rabbit chirruped impatiently, and I squinted through the glare to my right.

Then the light blinked out. I was thrust into pitch black.

I waited for my eyes to adjust, my breathing seeming loud in the sudden silence. The first thing I could distinguish, as my eyes became used to the sudden darkness, was the outline of the rabbit. Pale at first, it gradually became brighter.

It hopped impatiently away, but I needed a few more moments to get my bearings.

"Wait!" I called. It stopped, sat back and washed its whiskers, dutifully waiting for me while I gathered my senses.

Finally, I began to discern more of my surroundings. It was dark, yes, as though it were night here. But gradually, almost as though someone were twisting a dimmer switch, the buildings around me began to take shape.

Houses. A similar size and shape to Packhorse Close. Fairly even in height, from a distance these structures appeared newer, somehow less sunken than the ones on the other side of the wall. Doorknockers glowed dimly in the subdued light, as though the residents took pride in their humble abodes. Here and there, lamps were burning in windows. Other windows emitted a glow from behind closed curtains. I thought I could hear the faint tinkling of a piano.

*Plinkity-plonk.*

The wail of a baby.

Laughter.

Ordinary sounds.

They should have been a comfort, yet my scalp began to crawl.

In the distance, ahead of me, I recognised the familiar chiming of a clock. A big one. Like the one in the dome on the top of the Ministry of Witches building. Except—

I turned in place, listening hard. The clock's chimes were definitely coming from ahead of me and to the left, but the Ministry of Witches building should have been behind me and to the right. That seemed weird. I couldn't think of anywhere else with a clock of that size and magnitude in Tumble Town.

And *what* was it chiming anyway? I hadn't been paying proper attention, but I guessed I'd heard at least ten chimes. Or eleven. Perhaps even twelve.

That couldn't be. On the other side of the wall, just moments before, it hadn't even been twelve midday.

I pulled my mobile out of my pocket. The screen was blank. Pressing the on switch, I waited for it to warm up, listening out for the bing bongs as it came alive.

But the bing bongs never came. My phone was dead.

I tutted. A few paces ahead of me, the rabbit had finished its ablutions and begun to chirrup at me once more. I glanced over at it. This time when it hopped away, I followed.

There didn't seem much else I could do. I'd made my choice when I walked through 'the hole'.

"Go on then," I told it. "Show me what it is you want me to see."

If I'd hoped for a quick outcome to the white rabbit's puzzling behaviour, it didn't appear that one would be forthcoming. I trailed it all the way to the end of the lane, where Packhorse Way met another road as narrow as it was. We turned left. And a quick right. Then walked on for quite a long way. Then left. And right again.

I glimpsed a tavern down a narrow alley, its windows bright. I heard raucous jeering. Men and women. Someone exploded through the door, rapidly followed by someone else, and they began to scuffle. The sound of piano music followed them out.

*Plinkity-plonk. Plinkity-plonk.*

And more laughter.

In the darkness, I didn't recognise where I was, but I was used to the narrow lanes by now and the twisty-turny nature of Tumble Town. It wasn't until I reached a lane that seemed oddly familiar to me that I paused. Tall and narrow buildings. Slate roofs.

I retraced my steps around twenty feet or so to read the street sign above my head.

Artisan Lane?

I did a double take and then trailed after the rabbit, peering more closely at the store fronts here, looking out for something familiar. Except, where previously all of the stores had had glass windows with lively displays, and the general demeanour had been one of prosperity, now it felt almost run-down. Not old and decrepit the way parts of Tumble Town were, not derelict and neglected, just … like there wasn't a whole lot of money being spent here.

I frowned at the wooden front of a carpenter's shop. A simple bakery. A confectioner with an ornate display of chocolates, naked without any colourful bling. The rabbit skipped on, unaware of my confusion, and belatedly I twisted my head, searching for Bewitching Inks, but I must have missed it because I couldn't see its luminescent window anywhere.

*This is so strange,* I thought. I came through the wall and I should have been travelling in the opposite direction to this. I felt oddly disorientated, but I dutifully followed the rabbit up and down the now undulating landscape, following the curl of the road until we came to the narrow inlet that signified a set of steps I remembered far too well.

*Providence Steps.*

We had somehow doubled back on ourselves. It made no sense to me. Why bother with the whole rabbit hole thing if we'd simply ended up somewhere I already knew?

The rabbit hopped up the first couple of steps, stopped, and turned to look at me, a question in its eyes.

I pulled a face. "I really don't know about this," I told it. Memories of my previous ascent and even more rapid descent had rather dissuaded me against a repeat of the experience.

The rabbit chirruped, sounding more than a little annoyed.

"I'm assuming you want me to go back to Mr Culpeper's," I said, "but I really can't imagine he would be best pleased to see me again."

The rabbit squeaked, and this time there was no mistaking its anger.

I considered my options. I didn't have that many. Either I followed the rabbit, or I turned around and went home. I supposed I could either go directly back to the office or my flat or I could return to Packhorse Way. At the moment, I wasn't entirely sure why I would want to do any of those things.

But I couldn't help feeling confused. Confused about what time it was. Confused about the direction I had taken. I didn't feel as though my internal compass was working the way it should be. The only thing I wasn't confused about was my current location.

I took a deep breath as the rabbit squeaked again. "Alright! Alright!" It hopped up the next few steps and, reluctantly, I followed it. "Let's get to the bottom of this, shall we?"

The steps seemed easier to climb this time. Someone had been along and swept away the dead leaves and rubbish and weeded between the cracks. And the steps themselves didn't seem as worn. I watched where I was placing my feet, but every now and then peered up into the distance to check for anyone coming down towards me.

Nobody did.

We were about halfway to our destination when it occurred to me that besides the pair of revellers I'd seen bursting out of the tavern, we hadn't actually happened upon another living soul. And even the drunks had only been seen from a distance.

I'd *heard* people, but I hadn't come face to face with anyone.

I shook off the strangeness of that and climbed on, following the rabbit, wheezing heavily with the effort of the haul up the steep hill. Not quite soon enough for me, the little turning to the right materialised out of the darkness. I paused to catch my breath, thankful to have a moment, and studied my surroundings.

The last time I'd been here, I'd imagined Buckingham Place to be one of the dingiest alleys Tumble Town had to offer. Tonight—or whatever time it was— the darkness much improved matters. The tiny houses were still crowded together, and the space between opposite front doors was still ridiculously narrow, but the general gloom hid the filth, and the crumbling plaster was not so apparent.

The smell of woodsmoke filled the air and was far from unpleasant. It reminded me of my childhood. A secure feeling that had me longing for my mother. I descended the path towards where I remembered Culpeper's to be, imagining that it, like all the other shops I'd passed since leaving Packhorse Way, would be closed up for the night. But in the distance, I spotted a light glowing warmly in the large window, illuminating my path to the front door.

I glanced at the boxed-in window display area as I approached. The same hookah pipe sparkled in the space. A trick of the light made me believe it was smoking, but that couldn't be.

I paused in front of the door, the rabbit at my feet. It was late. What should I do? General etiquette meant I wouldn't normally be calling as late as this but, this evening, circumstances dictated otherwise.

I tapped on the solid wood with a smart rat-a-tat-tat. I might as well *pretend* to be confident, even if I wasn't entirely certain what sort of reception Mr Culpeper would afford me. When there was no response, I turned the big old-fashioned brass knob and pushed. The door swung smoothly on its hinges and I stepped forward into the small, dark room.

I sensed rather than saw the man in the shadows.

"Welcome back, Elise," came the quiet voice. "Mmm. I've been expecting you."

The scratch and hiss of a match was quickly followed by a bright flare of light. Mr Culpeper lit his lamp and slid it across the counter, effectively casting himself in the shadows once more.

"Welcome to the Ministry of Witches Police Department, Tumble Town Division."

I gaped at him, his pale face masked by flickering shadows. "You're …? Wait. What?"

"Mmm, yes." A deep chuckle. "The Dark Squad by, mmm, any other name."

CHAPTER 18

The Dark Squad?

The revelation was such a total surprise, my head involuntarily jerked backwards.

"That rather surprises you, mmm?"

"I have to confess, it does." I stepped a little closer to the counter, trying to get a better look at him. "Why all the subterfuge? The wall? The rabbits?"

"Not rabbits." Culpeper emphasised the S. "Rabbit. Just the one." He stretched out the long fingers of his right hand to indicate the white rabbit at my feet. His fingernails were long and ragged, the beds dark purple verging on black as though he had trapped them in a drawer. "DC Minsk here is a dedicated member of our team."

I shifted my gaze down to the rabbit. Minsk? I couldn't help feeling dubious. A rabbit detective?

"Mmmm." Culpeper chuckled. "The Dark Squad draw recruits from every faction open to them.

Including magickal animals, shapeshifters and devoted familiars."

"And which is Minsk?" I asked.

"Mmm? Whichever you want her to be."

Her? *Oops.* I had no idea why I'd been imagining she was a he.

"I'm not sure I want her to be anything." I peered down at the rabbit again. She narrowed her eyes. "No offence," I told her. "I'm not the sort of witch who utilises familiars, and I, er … can't afford any more partners."

"That's a shame," Culpeper said. "Minsk would be happy to work with you."

"Please can you explain what's going on?" I asked. "I stepped through the wall which I imagine was some sort of portal. I've heard stories about the number of portals in Tumble Town. But my sense of direction—which is generally quite good—tells me I was heading west, whereas Buckingham Place is in the east of the city. It feels like my inner roadmap has been reversed."

"Mmm. That's very astute of you, Elise."

"Everything is the same and yet subtly different." I frowned. "Now I think about it, it all seems somehow newer, but old. If that makes sense? Like I've stepped back in time. And it's night."

"Is that so?"

"Possibly twelve hours ahead of … or behind where I was," I continued, more to myself than to him, tipping my head back, lost in thought. "Like the world's been reversed or …" It came to me like a bolt out of the blue. "I've entered a reflection of my world!"

"Mmm. A reflection of a sort, yes. It is a portal, as you surmise. It's a copy of Tumble Town as you know it. The portal was created over one hundred and sixty years ago, and the world here is frozen in the same few moments. They play over and over again."

*How peculiar.* "Why?"

"It allows the Dark Squad to operate entirely in a different dimension. We can move between your world and this. And …"

"And others," I finished for him. I could only dream of such freedom. The idea of doing so seemed at once exhilarating and terrifying. What if you ended up stuck somewhere you didn't want to be?

"Exactly."

"So, nobody knows who you are or where you're based." I nodded with grudging admiration. "You're not renowned for being the friendly face of policing, no offence, and I suppose removing yourself from public view has some distinct advantages."

"Mmm. You are as smart as we imagined."

"Familiarity breeds contempt," I said. "And because you need to keep some of the residents of Tumble Town on their toes, I'd imagine not being around and becoming familiar works to your advantage."

Culpeper bobbed briefly into view. I had a vague impression that he was smiling, then he disappeared into the shadows once more. "Mmm. Quite so. We've been aware of you and your operation for some time. It was decided that we should issue you with an invitation to come here. It was Minsk's job to lead you."

"But I saw her a few days before I even knew Pack-horse Close existed. She led me to Makepeace."

"This is true. Minsk was tasked with leading you to him. When we found out about his death, we realised it might impinge on one of our own historical investigations—"

"I knew it!" I sang. "I've been telling Monk— DCI Wyld all along that there was a difference in the murders. You're investigating the bodies found in doorways in Packhorse Close. Am I right?"

"Mmm. In a manner of speaking." I heard some hesitation in his voice. "There are some things I cannot share with you, unfortunately. But, yes. It is our strongly held belief that the miserable demise of DC Makepeace is not linked to our case. We felt it only proper that we attended to our investigation and left you—or your side—to investigate the DC's regrettable death."

"We haven't progressed very far."

"No fault of yours, I imagine. We've been watching you. We're impressed with the way you work."

I wasn't sure how to react to that. It was nice that people had noticed me and my investigative agency, but I didn't like the idea of being watched. "Who do you mean by 'we'?" I wanted to know.

Culpeper bobbed around in the shadows. "Mmm. Me. My boss. The Chief Constable."

*Wow.* I could only imagine the Chief Constable of Tumble Town would be a fearsome spectacle. I wondered whether it was a he or a she. Not that it mattered. I'd probably never have any dealings with them.

"We wanted to chat with you, which is why Minsk came looking for you the second time. It is lamentable that this just happened to coincide with the dumping of another body."

Dumping?

"There was no intention on our part that you would stumble across the murder, although to be fair to Minsk, you didn't. She did."

*Semantics.*

"Mmm. Obviously being you," Culpeper continued, "you were side-tracked by the finding and alerted your own authorities before we could make a move to stop you. That wasn't ideal. We've been working hard over the decades to expunge the records relating to this case."

My head was spinning. "But why?"

"Because we can't afford to have the Rabbit Hole investigated properly. Increasingly, it's at risk of becoming the worst-kept secret in Tumble Town."

"But you know who is dumping the bodies in Pack-horse Close, don't you?" I asked. "If you're investigating whoever it is, why don't you arrest them and put an end to it?"

"It's not that simple. Mmm. If only it was."

"What do you mean?"

"Mmmm." Culpeper lapsed into silence.

Minsk shifted at my feet. "You promised you were going to warn her," she said, so quietly that at first, I didn't realise she had spoken.

"Telling her anything endangers her. It endangers all of us," Culpeper answered.

I stared down at the rabbit. "You can talk?"

She tutted. "Of course I can talk. And breathe. And think at the same time. Imagine that."

Snarky. I liked that. I hid a grin. "My apologies. I didn't mean—"

"Ah, save it," she said and twitched her ears. "You've enough to worry about."

I didn't like the turn this conversation was taking. "What do you mean?" I turned back to Culpeper. "Why am I in danger?"

Culpeper made a rasping, irritated sound in the back of his throat. There was a long silence. I waited. My heart beat a little harder.

Eventually, Culpeper slipped backwards. I heard a soft click. "Brief her, Minsk." He faded from view.

Minsk edged in front of me to issue instructions. "Push the counter on the right above me here. There should be a little catch." I did as she asked, and a door flipped open. There wasn't much room behind the counter and I half expected to find myself snuggling up with Culpeper, but there was no sign of him. He'd completely disappeared.

Minsk had followed me through, and now she pressed against the skirting board at my feet. The same soft click I'd heard before. Minsk butted her head against the wall to my right and another door opened, set slightly back from the continuing wall on the other side of the counter. No wonder I hadn't seen it.

I followed the rabbit down a narrow flight of steps,

the doors closing softly behind us. We descended into a corridor lined floor to ceiling with dark, smoky glass, occasionally broken up by a door. I had a sneaking suspicion that the glass acted like a two-way mirror. That the people behind it could see me, even though I couldn't see them. The architecture down here was the total opposite of what I expected from the ramshackle building above. Here, it was contemporary with sleek lines, beautifully sanded blonde wood to contrast the glass, the plaster freshly painted white.

Minsk stopped in front of one of the doors. "Push," she told me.

I did so. It opened with hardly a whisper. She hopped forward, the lights blinking on, subtly illuminating the office space rather than bleaching the room out with fluorescents. There were a number of desks in here, clear of the usual clutter you might expect to find on a workstation.

Well, you would at Wonderland, in any case. No Newton's Cradles here.

But it was the images all over the walls that caught my attention. The usual photographs of evidence and places, people and weapons that any homicide team would be familiar with. But the locus among these was a large poster-sized image of a labyrinth that took pride of place dead centre of the display.

Mouth open, I made a beeline for it and tapped it. "I've seen this," I told Minsk. "As a tattoo."

Minsk hopped up onto a chair. "I figured you might have."

"What does it mean? Does it denote a group of some kind?"

"In a manner of speaking, although cult might be a better word for them."

I raised an eyebrow.

"It's a symbol used by an organisation called The Labyrinth Society, an old adversary of ours. In fact, it's likely that the seeds of The Labyrinth Society go back several hundred years, perhaps even more to the Middle Ages. Nobody quite knows for sure."

I nodded and began studying other images on the wall. Some of them did not make for pretty viewing. Corpses. Lots of violence.

"When the Ministry of Witches first put a tentative foot into the waters of policing, there was—understandably perhaps—a wave of negativity from the wider community. But back in the eighteen fifties, Tumble Town was entirely lawless. It was a grim place to live. There needed to be some order, and so the Ministry of Witches persisted. They commandeered a number of buildings in Tumble Town to use as police stations and recruited decent officers. But time and time again, the buildings were burned down, the fleeing officers were set upon and …" Minsk took a breath. "I'm sure you can guess the rest."

I shuddered. I could imagine.

"The Ministry of Witches were at their wits' end. They considered pulling the MOWPD out of Tumble Town but didn't want to admit defeat, and losing face to these bullies was out of the question. Imagine the consequences!"

I nodded. It wouldn't have been a good look.

"And so, a number of great wizards were called upon to come up with a solution."

"They created the Rabbit Hole?"

"Exactly. Even now, I think it was one of the single most magnificent magickal acts the world has ever known, on our plane at least."

"It kept the police safe, and they couldn't be hounded." Sounded perfect to me.

"Precisely. Unfortunately, the worst villains weren't happy at all. Now the Dark Squad—as our branch of the MOWPD rapidly became known—went after murderers and swindlers as soon as they had enough evidence to proceed. There was retaliation, of course—"

"The Labyrinth Society?"

"That's where it gets interesting. Back in the eighteen fifties, we had no idea that such a criminal organisation existed, but we became aware of people searching for the Rabbit Hole. One of the wizards who had been instrumental in setting up the magickal force field that cut Packhorse Way in two was tortured and murdered. We could never be sure how much information he gave away, but the fact remains that ever since then, there have been numerous attempts to access the Rabbit Hole, and some of them have resulted in glitches in the magickal field."

"Glitches?"

"Think of the magickal field as a fabric that holds the Rabbit Hole together, frozen in time. Occasionally, parts of that fabric get worn. They fray. This is a weakness that needs to be rectified as soon as it's identified.

We have a team of wizards in a secret location—well away from Tumble Town itself—working around the clock to keep the whole thing together. The Labyrinth Society are constantly on the lookout for those glitches, and somehow—we don't know how—they can tell where they are and when they occur. We're constantly on the back foot, reacting to what they do, trying to plug the holes."

Minsk hopped down from her chair and scampered to the corner of the room where a long, thin stick leaned against the wall. She picked it up and tipped her head back, searching the images until she found the one she was looking for, and banged the tip of the stick against it. "Take a look at her."

I did as she asked, getting in close to examine the photo. A woman. In her seventies, perhaps. A headscarf wrapped around her head, knotted under the neck. She looked somehow familiar. "Do I know her?"

"You've passed her a few times."

"Passed her?" Suddenly it came to me. "The woman on the steps! Providence Steps. She's a glitch?"

"That's right."

"I knew there was something weird about her."

"The glitch in the magick program there allows The Labyrinth Society a limited amount of access from their Tumble Town plane to our private one." She tipped her head up to look at me. "Imagine someone putting the tip of their finger into a small tear in their clothing. If they keep worrying at it, the tear becomes larger. Eventually you would be able to put your finger through, then your whole hand and so on. We're constantly repairing it, but it's an ongoing battle."

"I see."

I could only assume that The Labyrinth Society had been responsible for pushing me down the steps. I'd been fortunate that Mr Culpeper had been able to reach out and rescue me without physically being there.

Thank the goddess for him.

"The bodies in Packhorse Close. Who are they? How are they related to all this?"

"That's a little complicated." Minsk returned her pointer to its place in the corner. "The Labyrinth Society is highly secretive. Underground as the name suggests. Beyond our reach. There are several off-shoots of the society, which—according to our intelli-gence—acts as a kind of umbrella organisation. The people who work for it are widely known as Labyrinthians, and every person recruited to its ranks receives a tattoo."

"Do you know who the artist is?" I asked, wondering how Kevin Makepeace was linked to all this.

"No. We have no knowledge of who the tattoo artist is, although we've been trying to find him. We think he moves premises. We don't have the resources to keep throwing at a moving target."

"It seems to me if you knew who he was, he'd be a link to The Labyrinth Society," I said. That didn't personally strike me as a waste of resources. I'd see it as a potential way in. Presumably, the Dark Squad had bigger fish to fry.

"We've been concentrating our recent efforts on a

primary subgroup known as 'the Bulls'. They're fronted by several ne'er-do-wells and cause us a huge headache because of their mobility. They're men, mostly, although we have some intelligence that a number of younger women have become involved with them. The Bulls are rough. Pretty hardcore."

"They sound a little intimidating," I agreed.

"Yes. They can be. They're Labyrinthian soldiers, if you like. They like to fight."

"And these are the ones who turn up dead in the doorway of Packhorse Close?" That didn't make a lot of sense to me. Why would someone be killing the Bulls outside the Rabbit Hole? Unless—

My mouth dropped open in horror. "You guys are killing them?"

Minsk reeled away from me. "Good goddess, no! We wouldn't do that. You well know that magicide is the most serious of crimes!"

"I don't get it, then."

"It's not *us* who're killing these men, it's the Bulls."

Now I was more confused than ever. "Why would the Bulls kill their own?"

"Because they're not *their* own. They're *ours*."

What was she saying? "*Yours?*" I grasped her meaning and my breath caught in my throat. "They were undercover?"

Minsk nodded, her ears drooping. "It's become routine for us to send some of our best young recruits undercover in Tumble Town, in the hope that they'll get a lead and wangle their way into the Labyrinth Society somehow. Over the years, we've become adept at choosing the right sort of recruits. Curious, confident, clean cut. Tough. Overwhelmingly male. But the Labyrinthians have become ever more suspicious and occasionally, heartbreakingly, they leave us a gift at the entrance to the Rabbit Hole."

I swallowed. As an ex-serving officer, that was difficult to hear.

"Was Kevin Makepeace one of yours?" I asked.

"No." Minsk's response was both quick and firm.

"But he had the tattoo," I said.

Minsk's whiskers twitched. "Are you sure?"

"Exactly the same as the one the other bodies had. The only difference between them was location."

"And the fact that ours were Dark Squad," Minsk reminded me. "Your man was definitely not one of ours."

"His tattoo was fresh," I recalled. "Only a few days old. Perhaps he had been recruited to the Bulls?"

"That's a possibility. And if they found out he was MOWPD, his days would have been numbered."

I turned to examine the wall of evidence once more. A large taped-off section had been given over to mugshots of officers, missing, presumed dead. Such young faces, no older than Wootton.

Icy fingers wrapped themselves around my heart. "If the Labyrinthians know I've been poking around, presumably they know who I am and what I do."

"Almost certainly."

"They targeted me, on Providence Steps." I brushed my hair away from my face, a nervous tic. "Would they target my staff too?"

Minsk stared at me. "Possibly."

"One of my staff is missing," I said. "He thought he would meet me in Packhorse Close, but he hasn't been seen for over twenty-four hours."

Minsk started. "That's not good." She hopped towards the door. "I'll need his details. We'll circulate the information but—"

"But?" I asked, my voice rising in alarm.

"Chances are—" she stopped and tilted her head up to look at me, her chocolate eyes warm and yet bleak at the same time. I'd seen that look before. Heck, I'd probably *worn* that look before, whenever I shared bad news with unsuspecting relatives.

She didn't need to say anything else.

I swallowed.

The chances were that attacking Wootton would be a warning to me to back off.

The chances were, he would turn up in a doorway near Wonderland very soon.

Covered in a sleeping bag.

Dead.

CHAPTER 19

"There must be something we can do. Some way we can find him." I hurried after Minsk as she tore down the corridor.

"Push," she told me as we reached another glass door.

I did as she asked and followed her into a dark hub that looked more like a NASA control centre than anything I'd ever found in a police station on my side of the Rabbit Hole. There were rows of desks, operatives sitting at each with headphones on, staring at screens and rapidly typing away. Apart from the glow from the screens, there was little lighting in here—most of it concentrated at the front half of the room where people were working. Towards the rear, the shadows were thick, but I spotted movement around a table. People who did not want to be seen.

"Selwyn?" Minsk rose on her back legs and placed her paws on one man's thigh. "I need you to circulate the details of a missing person. He's been gone over

183

twenty-four hours and is likely a person of interest for the Labyrinthians."

"No problem," Selwyn nodded. "Do we have a description?"

I stepped in and described Wootton to the best of my ability. Tall and lanky, dark haired, elf-eared.

"A photo would be a great help." Selwyn blinked up at me. I fumbled for my phone and quickly scrolled through the images in my gallery. I found a good one taken not so long ago, on the opening day of Wonderland. We'd retired to the Pig and Pepper, where I'd introduced Ezra to the rest of the gang. Wootton, slightly tipsy probably, was beaming into the camera.

Selwyn pulled out some kind of electronic wand, tapped my phone and instantly Wootton's barmy smile was projected onto several screens at the front of the room. He attacked his keyboard again, firing words into the ether. Wootton's image glowed softly on every screen, pulsed a couple of times, then popped and disappeared.

"Gone," said Selwyn. "All of our officers and operatives will be on the lookout for him now. Information will be gathered here centrally. We'll let you know if there's any news." He peered down at Minsk for approval.

"Thank you," she said and headed back to the exit.

"Wait," I called. "That's it? Isn't there something else I can do?"

"Like what?" Minsk asked. "You know as well as anyone, it's just a matter of hanging tight—"

"No," I said, my voice firm—and loud in the calm

atmosphere of the control room. "I was worried about Wootton before, but after this whole—" I wasn't quite sure what to call it. I indicated the room and gestured around at the building and shrugged, lost for words. "After this whole shizazz, after all you've told me, and knowing there are people out there who more than likely mean him harm—"

"Be calm, DI Liddell," Minsk urged me.

"How can I?" I asked, totally infuriated.

"Mmmm. DI Liddell?" Culpeper's voice drifted out of the shadows. Evidently, he was one of those loitering at the rear of the room.

I pulled myself together. "My apologies." I wouldn't explain to them about Ezra, about how the fear of losing someone else was a constant anxiety gnawing at my innards.

"There is a way you may be able to, mmmm, assist us," Culpeper said. I spotted Minsk's frown. "If you're willing."

"Anything," I replied.

"You want me to go undercover?" I almost laughed. "It's been a while since I did any undercover work. A few years, in fact."

Minsk and I had joined Culpeper in a dark ante-room. He hung back. I still couldn't make him out, just an occasional glance of his pale face. This discrete space allowed us a little more privacy and meant we weren't disturbing anyone in the control room.

"Mmmm. I'm sure it will come back to you," Mr Culpeper said. "I've had a word with my superior, and he's given me the go-ahead to try my idea out."

They wanted me to be some young hip and trendy type. I scrunched my face up, thinking rapidly. "Don't you think I'm a bit long in the tooth?"

"You're on the cusp of what I would consider acceptable," Minsk nodded. "But with a little more moisturiser and some thicker concealer, nobody will notice you're looking a little rough around the edges."

"Thank you very much," I grumbled.

"You've already done most of the hard work by visiting so many tattoo parlours. All we need is for you to switch personas. Instead of a detective, you'll be looking for receptionist work. We need you to stay long enough in each of the places you visit to get a look at the premises, as far as possible anyway."

"Mmm. Just flag any that you find a little suspicious, and we'll take over from there."

"What exactly would you call suspicious?" I had my own ideas of what constituted weird, and unfortunately, that accounted for about eighty per cent of all Tumble Town residents as far as I could see.

"We're after the tattooist," Minsk reminded me. "The one who creates the labyrinths."

"I understand that," I said. "But if I was a tattooist working for an underground organisation, I'd hide what I did out of plain sight."

"It probably is out of sight, yes, but there might be activity that you find suspicious. Lots of people coming and going. The owner behaving shiftily …"

186

I didn't find much solace in her words. I found most people in Tumble Town shifty.

"You'll have to trust your instincts," Minsk told me.

"I can do that." I'd had to on numerous occasions while working for the MOWPD. Detectives grew a thick skin and an unerring nose for things that weren't quite right.

"Mmmm. We've concocted a new CV for you to take around to various businesses. I've enlisted the help of one of our current operatives, Nimrod Bodovsky from Bewitching Inks. I believe you m-m-m-may well have come across him."

The name didn't ring a bell.

"He has spiky hair," Minsk chipped in.

"A mmmowhawk," Mr Culpeper added.

Of course. Mohawk Man. He was part of the Dark Squad! You could have knocked me down with a feather. I hadn't found him a particularly appealing character, but now I thought about it, he'd been the one to signpost Mr Culpeper to me. Perhaps his lasciviousness had been all part of his undercover persona.

Or maybe he was just a creep.

"Yes, I remember him."

"He'll provide a reference," Culpeper said. "Mmm, a glowing one. You understand, however, that this is a risky mission. We'll have to take your phone and anything that would pertain to your real identity from you."

"I might need my phone," I argued.

"We'll give you one of ours. Mmm, Minsk?"

Minsk nodded. "Yes, good idea. You can have a

burner. Entirely untraceable. Dial five at any time and we will come in to get you, no matter where you are or what you're doing."

"What if someone recognises me?" I'd been in *The Celestine Times* not so long ago, plus the Labyrinthians were evidently aware of me; why else would they have tried to throw me down Providence Steps or have abducted Wootton?

"Beat it!" Minsk thumped her left rear leg on the floor. "Double time. Then call for help."

"Good advice. Run, Elise. As hard as you can. These people are not to be trifled with." Mr Culpeper's words induced even more anxiety. "Remember, mmm, we'll have numerous operatives in the area. Someone will always be on hand."

"That's reassuring." I took a deep breath. "Okay, let's do it."

"Not so fast," Minsk said, staring up at me with bright, shining eyes. "We'll need to have your appearance altered—"

"Hang on—" I hadn't signed up to that.

"Just a tad," Minsk added. I could have sworn she was smiling. "It won't take long."

"Mmmm, nothing to worry about," Mr Culpeper said. "Wizard Filigree is one of the finest forensic cosmetic alchemists in the business."

I closed my eyes. "Oh, cripes."

*What had I let myself in for?*

As it turned out, it wasn't so bad.

I'd heard rumours about cosmetic alchemy disasters, but Wizard Filigree turned out to be an interesting character in his own right. Dressed in black police robes, he was a handsome man in his early forties, with close-cropped hair, slightly greying at the temples, and eyes almost the same colour as Minsk's.

I'd changed into a hospital gown at his behest. Now he pointed at a tall stool beside the desk of his office-come-laboratory. "Take a seat, Ms Liddell."

I did as he asked, feeling a quiver in my stomach.

He angled a lamp towards me and pulled out a magnifying glass. "May I?"

"Of course." I had to stop myself from leaning away from him as he examined my skin with microscopic interest.

"You have good skin, although I suspect you may use alcohol a little too much," he told me in a blunt tone.

*Ouch.* "I've given it up." Eight weeks and three days. Not that I was counting.

He moved behind my head. "That's good." I heard the approval. "You don't smoke either."

"No."

"So that's a decent enough base for me to do what I need to do. Superintendent Culpeper has given me a brief based on the operation you're going to undertake for him. I'm actually not going to alter too much. Your hair is fine as it is. So, I think I'll change the shape of your eyes, throw on a few tattoos and piercings and leave it at that. The less we change, the better recovery is for you."

"Piercings?" I asked. "Is this going to hurt?"

Filigree smiled. "Nothing that a couple of paraceta-mols won't sort out."

"I'm not so sure—"

Filigree flipped a switch by the door. A large circular light blinked on above a chair at the side of the room. "Would you mind?" He indicated I should move over to what looked rather like a dentist's chair. As soon as I took a seat, it began to lie flat, pushing my feet up off the floor.

"I really don't—"

"Don't worry about a thing, it will be over in seconds." He busied himself, pulling on a pair of goggles and then dragging a screen around me. "The problem with both tattoos and piercings is that it's all about the needles."

I emitted a shrill giggle. "When I was a child, we used to have these stamps that you licked and slapped on your arm. Surely you have slightly more upmarket versions of those I could use?"

Filigree maintained his professionalism, but I sensed a certain weariness. "We need to do things to you that will look authentic to those who know about such things. Your tattoos can't be superficial—but don't worry, they will fade after a couple of washes."

"Good news," I muttered. Above my head, the light began to pulse, and a silver tube started to descend. I caught my breath. "What's that thing?"

"Relax, Ms Liddell, it's the laser. It does all the work."

*Meep!*

"I'm going to count down slowly from five, and the

process will begin. It will be over before you register that it's started. If you could remove your gown now, to expose your arms?"

I took a beat but realised there was no getting out of this. The sooner I did as he said, the better. I yanked the gown off, modestly covering my mid-bits and rolling my eyes.

"Five, four, three—"

He'd lied! This wasn't a slow count!

"—two, one!"

I grimaced.

*Zzzzzzzzzzzzzzzzzzzzzzzzzzippppppppppp.*

A blinding flash of light and one trillion needles—well, that's what it felt like—pierced my skin at once. I shrieked in pain and surprise, made a grab at my nose, and then … nothing.

"All done!" Wizard Filigree sang, far too cheerfully for my liking. "You can put your gown back on now."

I reached for my gown and stared down at my skin in surprise. I had full sleeve tattoos, one on each arm. Dark green ivy climbed gracefully up towards my shoulders, colourful birds flying around it. Crimson hearts bled black blood, having been impaled by deadly looking daggers. Chains interspersed gravestones.

"Wow, that's heavy stuff," I said, rubbing at the ink. I'd never wanted a tattoo, and here I was with dozens of them.

"How are you feeling?" Wizard Filigree pulled back the screen and I hurriedly covered myself.

"My nose is throbbing a bit," I said and put my hand back up, knocking something cold and smooth.

Filigree grabbed a mirror and handed it over. I stared in shock at my face. He'd said he would alter my eyes, and he had done. Where I'd considered them to be fairly ordinary, they had now taken on a feline curve. Added to that, they had been heavily rimmed with kohl. The whole effect should have aged me, but my skin was smooth and firm. I stroked my cheek appreciatively.

"Only temporary I'm afraid," Wizard Filigree said, "then it's back to the slightly saggy older skin."

I wondered if he was married. Who could put up with that level of honesty in their life? I'd have walked out on him forty-eight hours into the relationship.

I toyed with the piercing in my nose. The kind of ring they put through a bull's nose. There were also piercings in both eyebrows and, when I stuck my tongue out to find why that was stinging, too, I discovered a prong through it.

"Good gracious. That's hideous," I lisped.

Wizard Filigree did not take offence. "Perfect, isn't it? Even though I do say so myself. You'll look just the ticket."

"Am I going to be able to eat with that thing in?"

Filigree shrugged. "I, erm, I have no idea. Give it a go." His worried expression faded as a thought occurred to him. "Perhaps you could report back? In the interests of research, you know?"

"I'll bear it in mind," I muttered.

He pressed a button, and the overhead light blinked out as the chair began to resume a sitting position. As soon as my feet could touch the floor, I jumped up.

"Before you go—" Filigree's voice stopped me from

running from the room. "I have some painkillers if you think you'll need them?"

I paused and listened to my body. Some slight throbbing here and there, nothing I couldn't handle. "No, I'll be fine."

I made a dash for the door, keen to make my escape before he could jab me with anything else. As my hand turned the handle, I realised how churlish I was being. The poor wizard had a job to do. We were on the same side.

"Thanks for your help," I said. "Any other words of advice?"

"Try not to get caught in the rain too often."

## CHAPTER 20

Armed with a list of tattoo parlours to visit on the far east side of Tumble Town, Minsk escorted me to the Rabbit Hole.

"Once you step through, there's no coming back," she told me.

"I understand." My speech sounded odd to me, as though the prong through my tongue, or something else that Wizard Filigree had done, had altered the timbre of my voice somehow. "How will I report back?"

"Don't worry, we'll contact you." She sat back on her haunches and stared up at me. "Be careful out there, DI Liddell."

"Call me Elise, please," I told her. I wasn't sure we were friends, but she was ridiculously cute and I had a sudden urge to remain in contact. "You'll keep searching for Wootton, won't you?"

"I promise. And if we find him before you do, we'll pull you from this undercover case straight away. You appreciate how dangerous the Labyrinthians are, don't you?"

"I don't mind doing this—"

She raised a dinky paw. "I know. We appreciate all that you've volunteered to undertake for us, honestly. There's no need for you to be part of this at all. It's our problem. As far as I can see, there's no overlap between your case and ours."

I held my tongue. I wasn't so sure.

"Take care, Elise." She wiggled her whiskers, and the wall in front of us began to shimmer and spiral. Chinks of light appeared as bricks cracked and crumbled. When a big enough gap had formed, I stepped through it, blinking into the natural light—not bright sunlight by any means, but brighter than anything I'd experienced beyond the Rabbit Hole.

Stone ground itself against stone, and the earth beneath my feet shuddered. I turned to watch the wall slide back into place, the graffiti I recognised exactly where I'd expect it to be. Once it had fully closed, I crouched down, searching for the 'Push me' brick, seeking to reassure myself that if I wanted to, I could actually return.

But it seemed that neither the brick nor the instruction existed anymore.

My permission to travel beyond the Rabbit Hole had been well and truly revoked.

After the cacophonous row the wall had made as it closed behind me, the world seemed suddenly silent. In the distance, I heard the clock above the Ministry of

Witches chiming midday. Was this the same day? If so, I'd been gone hardly any time at all.

I began to pick my way through the litter, heading along the narrow passageway between the houses of Packhorse Close. I paused for a second outside number 67. Boarded up, the ancient paint on the wooden frames around the windows flaking away, I still had a sense that the place wasn't empty. Not entirely. Had I been Monkton, I'd have sent someone in to give it a proper once-over, but I wasn't him and it wasn't my place.

I picked up speed, eager to get away from that house, frightened someone would see me and recognise me for who I really was and report me to the Labyrinthians. As I passed Monkton's police officers, I turned my head away to avoid catching an eagle eye. Fortunately, their attention was being held by a confused old lady lambasting them for not attending her abode when she'd first reported a break-in back in 1983.

I paused at the end of the close where it joined with Cross Lane. I had to resist the temptation to race back to the relative safety of Wonderland. I couldn't afford to let anyone there know what I was doing. And if anybody was watching the office in Tudor Lane, me turning up in my current guise would be likely to give the game away.

No. I was on my own until I'd accomplished my mission or until Culpeper called me off. Whichever came first.

"Go, go, go!" A soft voice in the shadows.

Startled, I whirled to peer into the gloomy doorway. Nothing there.

"And take care!" The same voice—from behind me this time.

Unnerved, I hurried away, ignoring the chortle of laughter that drifted after me.

The first tattoo parlour I approached had been imaginatively named Dream Masters. It bore a striking resemblance to Bewitching Inks on Artisan Lane, with its gaudy displays and bright neon lights. I pushed through the heavy door and found myself in a space that might have doubled as a nightclub. Industrial rock music blared out through enormous speakers, drowning out the buzzing of ink guns and everything else.

A bored receptionist leaned against the front counter picking black varnish from her nails and chewing gum. I reached into my bag and whisked out a copy of my CV and covering letter.

"Is your boss in?" I asked.

She looked up from below her eyelashes, not giving me the benefit of her full face. "You what?" she mouthed.

"Is your boss in?" I yelled.

She tutted—not that I could hear it, I could just tell by the face she pulled—and jerked a thumb towards the back.

I wasn't sure what she was suggesting I do. Stay where I was or go and find him. I decided, given that I was short on time, I would go and find him. It would allow me an opportunity to have a look around, at any rate.

I moved past the reception desk and walked through to the business part of the shop floor. One of the tattooists glanced up as I skirted his chair.

"Hey!" I heard the receptionist shout after me. Evidently, she hadn't meant I should go and find her boss myself after all.

My bad.

I nodded at the tattooist, who smiled back—he was wearing a gold grill on his bottom teeth—and continued my journey through to the rear of the shop. There were three identical doors there, but they had been handily labelled with hand-painted signs. One had a bathroom sign, one had a sign saying 'Private' and the final one said 'Office'.

I opted for the office.

I lifted my hand to knock on the door just as the receptionist caught up with me. "You can't go in there!" she shouted at me.

"You told me I could!" I yelled back.

She grabbed for my arm as I reached for the handle. I shook her off.

"No, you can't!" She yanked at me. This time I elbowed her hard, connecting with her chin. She howled and retreated.

Free at last, I yanked open the door.

A middle-aged man, salt and pepper hair, wearing smart robes, shot upright in surprise as I appeared in his doorway. His nose was coated in white powder, the same stuff he had lined up on his desk, I suppose.

"What do you want?" he snarled, a curled twenty-pound note in his hand.

"A job?" I said.

"We're not hiring. Get lost!"

I nodded. "My mistake."

Back out on the street, I had to giggle to myself. I had half a mind to report the owner to the MOWPD drug enforcement team but decided, given my undercover status, it would be wiser to move right along.

*Nothing to see here.*

I visited another couple of businesses close by, and in both cases found decent enough premises and pleasant staff. There were no vacancies anywhere, but more importantly, neither of them gave me cause for suspicion.

I grabbed a coffee from a small sandwich shop near the southern end of Tumble Town, on my way towards Dead Man's Wharf. Checking the list Culpeper had furnished me with, a hastily drawn map of roads and alleys on the reverse, I realised that the next business I needed to investigate was close by in an adjacent street. If I'd wanted to, I could have taken a narrow ginnel through to Tetris Alley, but I decided to exercise caution and walk the long way around. It wouldn't take much time—and the streets, while not devoid of passers-by, weren't busy.

This business, Wasted Youth Tattoos of East Tumble Town, was a far cry from Dream Masters. No neon lighting here. No disco ball or loud music. Just a couple of faded posters in the window—along with some dead and desiccated wasps—and mesh covering the door.

I peered through the grimy glass. I couldn't see a whole lot. I was probably wasting my time, but given that the business was next on the list, I felt compelled to pay a visit and tick it off.

I pushed the door. It swung open easily enough, revealing a small room. The proprietor, because I assumed that's who it was, was sprawled back on the only inking station in the whole place. He opened one eye and tipped his head up to get a better look at me.

"Hel-lo darling," he said and leapt up with an explosive burst of energy.

I couldn't help but perk up a little myself. This guy was eye-candy, sister! Slightly older than me, he had long, reddy-blond wavy hair down to his waist and boy, was he buff. He had on a tight pair of faded denims, a pair of cowboy boots that might even have been genuine and a leather waistcoat. And that, my friends, was pretty much it. Nicely tanned, in a way unusual among Tumble Town residents, he had muscles on his muscles and a washboard stomach to boot. If he'd been wearing furs, he might have passed for a moustache-less Viking.

"Are you here for a tattoo?" he asked, raising his eyebrows hopefully.

Darn it. He might have changed my mind about not wanting one.

"I, erm, no," I said slowly. "I was rather hoping you might have a job going."

"Oh." His face fell. He gestured around. "As you can see, this is strictly a one-man affair."

I nodded, taking my time to survey my surroundings. Nothing untoward.

"You're an artist?" he was asking.

I shook my head. "I was rather hoping for a receptionist's position." I flapped my CV at him. "I have experience."

"I'm sure you do," he grinned. The double entendre wasn't lost on me.

"And references."

"Where have you worked?"

"At Bewitching Inks with Nimrod," I lied.

He nodded, considering this. "Nimrod is a good man, yeah."

There was something about the way he said that—almost casually, and yet with some hidden meaning—that caused a frisson of alarm to pulse through my insides. "He is," I replied.

"I couldn't work with Ivor though," the Viking said. "He's a complete fruit and nutcase."

My heart sped up. What was the correct response? Was there an Ivor at Bewitching Inks? There had been another man working there. He might be Ivor. Dang and blast. This is what comes of going undercover without being properly prepared.

*Trust your instincts*, Culpeper had said.

"Ivor?" I repeated, affecting an air of puzzlement. "I don't recall an Ivor."

"You don't?" The Viking sucked his teeth. "I could have sworn—hmm—my mistake."

My knees shook with relief. I waved my CV again and shrugged. "Well, I'm sorry to have wasted your time."

"Not at all." He held my gaze. "Was it only work in tattoo parlours you were looking for?"

"No, anything really. I'm at a loose end, you know how it is." I resisted the urge to squirm.

"Yeah." His eyes dropped to study the tattoos on my arms. "Nice work. Did Nimrod do those?"

"Some of them. I had a friend do most of the work." *More of an acquaintance, really.*

He nodded, slowly, then stepped closer and held his hand out for my CV. "If I hear anything, I'll let you know."

I didn't want to hand it over.

"I presume your phone number is on this."

"Yes, it is." Not my real one, but one that would connect to the Dark Squad's operations room where someone would pretend to be me. It would seem churlish if I didn't give the envelope to him. After a beat, I did so.

"Thanks for your time," I said, backing towards the door.

"No problem." He saluted me with the envelope, a curl of amusement to his lips.

I pushed out of the door, feeling a wave of relief as it gently clanged shut behind me. Taking a couple of large gulps of fresh air, I turned my head up to the sky. The sun had set behind the houses, but I still had a couple of businesses on my list to visit.

Unsure whether to turn left or right, I decided to

head back to the sandwich shop and get my bearings, but as I walked past the shop window, I had a definite sense of the Viking watching me. I half turned, then thought better of it. How would it seem if I glanced back at him?

I hurried to the corner of the road, out of sight of the shop, and fumbled in my bag for my phone. Something wasn't quite right. I couldn't put my finger on what, not exactly, but Culpeper had been adamant that I should report any small thing that gave me concern. I decided I would call him.

Pulling the burner phone out of my bag, I examined the screen. It was a simple thing, no whistles and bells. I hit the five button and started to lift the phone to my ear.

"Beware," someone said. A voice in the gloom to my right.

"Be wary," agreed a papery voice to my left.

Too late!

Hands were reaching for me. An arm around my neck, cutting off my breath. Somebody yanked the phone from my hand, and I heard the sound of plastic smashing on the rough paving followed by a crunch. As I struggled, trying to gain enough leverage to strike out with an elbow or a knee, my bag was snatched from my shoulder.

The arm around my neck slackened momentarily. "Uuuurggh!" I called out, as loud as I could manage, trying to swing myself around at the same time. A heavy fist slammed into my chin.

I would have dropped to the floor had someone not

been holding me up. Stars floated in my vision for a few seconds and the world greyed out, a whiny buzz causing my head to throb. Momentarily I became heavy, until a little strength crept back into my limbs. When I could see and hear again, I realised I was being half carried, half dragged down a tiny side alley. I could smell the river and hear the faint sounds of water sloshing against buildings.

The man holding me up paused. My head wobbled on my shoulders as I tried to see what was happening. In front of me, someone was banging on a door. Almost immediately, it opened.

"Hurry!"

I was bundled through a room, a kitchen perhaps; I could smell something cooking. Fish. Someone's dinner.

"Down there."

Another door. This one whined on its hinges. I was propelled through. In my slightly befuddled state, I could see there were steps down, wooden ones descending into the gloom. My abductor released his tight grip on my arm and thrust me forwards. I managed to hold my balance for half a dozen steps, but then I lost my footing and tumbled down the last six on my backside.

"Oof!" Breath exploded out of me. I landed in a sitting position at the foot of the stairs, certain I must have broken my hip or something. Less than a second later, the room was plunged into darkness as the door on its rusty hinges was slammed closed. I distinctly heard bolts being dragged into place.

"Not good," I muttered, tentatively shifting from buttock to buttock to test for breakages.

Something shuffled towards me. "Who's there?" I demanded.

Icy fingers reached out and clamped my wrist. I shrieked and leapt to my feet. "Back away!" I ordered, raising my hands, ready to perform some nifty jiu-witchtsu.

A small, familiar voice. "I'm W-wuh-Wootton."

"Wootton?" I could hardly believe it. My heart did a leap. I'd found him! "It's me! Elise! Are you alright? I can't see you."

"Yu-your eyes will get yu-used to the luh-light in a minute."

I reached for him anyway, finding him kneeling on the floor, his shoulders bony. I ran my palms down his arms until I found his ice-cold hands and clasped them in mine.

"You're freezing!"

"I've been down here for what feels like years. I'm suh-so cold."

"Here!" I stripped off my leather gilet. Only I would have agreed to go undercover without a decent coat or jacket. Even Alf's old robes would have been warmer than what Culpeper had given me as a 'disguise'.

And in the end, it had been worse than useless.

"Sorry, it's not much," I said, arranging it around his shoulders.

I found myself involuntarily shivering in my thin t-shirt. It wouldn't be long until I was as cold as Wootton, but as he'd said, my eyes were beginning to adjust to the gloom. I hauled him to his feet and pulled the gilet over him when it slipped, then dragged him to a corner. We sat side by side, huddled together, me sharing my body warmth with him.

"Can't you cast a spell and make it warm?" Wootton asked.

I snorted. "I'm not that sort of witch, mate. They took my bag and my wand. I guess if there was something to burn, a pile of wood or something, I might be able to light it."

"I haven't come across any. In fact, I haven't found anything much. And what I have found is so damp." He shivered again. "What about light? Can you turn on a light?"

I looked up towards the ceiling, but in the darkness I really couldn't see. I couldn't magick light from nothing. I decided it would be best to change the subject rather than raise Wootton's hopes.

"What happened to you?" I asked. "I've been worried sick!"

"I came to find you. I thought I had some useful information about the murders, so I followed you down to Packhorse Close—"

"Except I was going shopping to buy Snitch some new shoes."

"Oh." Wootton's laugh sounded hollow. "That's why I didn't find you."

"Sorry, I should have made it clear. I didn't imagine for a minute—"

"It's my fault. I should have stayed put."

"What happened?" I repeated. "How did they grab you?"

Wootton's trembling had eased somewhat. For now, at least, he was a little warmer.

"It was the weirdest thing. I walked down Packhorse Close and I could have sworn you were there. Or someone who looked just like you. You had your back to me, but your hair and leather jacket? It was you! Except someone came out of a doorway and distracted me, just momentarily. When I looked down the alley, you weren't there anymore, just some old woman pottering around outside one of the houses."

"Which house?"

Wootton shook his head. "I don't recall. It was towards the end of the row, relatively close to the wall."

"The last habitable dwelling on the left-hand side?" I asked.

Wootton thought for a moment. "Yes, could be. Do you know the woman I'm talking about?"

"No," I said, thinking of the wizard goblin I'd met there. There was something intriguing about that house. "I don't think so. Tell me about her."

"She was a wee bit ditsy. In her eighties. Maybe older. All hunched over. She thought I was coming to visit her. Kept asking me if I was her son. Quite clearly, her son would be in his fifties or sixties. I thought she was confused. I told her I was looking for my boss. She seemed harmless enough. I didn't think not to mention Wonderland or you ..."

"It's okay," I said. "How could you know?"

"I finally managed to extricate myself from the conversation. I could see you weren't there, so I bid her a polite goodbye and began to walk away. But she called me back. I turned around, just to be polite, and instead of her, there was this enormous guy. He decked me with one blow. After that, I don't remember a whole lot. I was carried … over his shoulder … and ended up here. It feels like I've been here for days. How long has it been?"

"Less than forty-eight hours."

Wootton fidgeted next to me and shivered again. "It's so cold down here. Do you think we're going to die?"

I freed my arm long enough to give him a soft punch. "What? No, we're not going to die!" I cast my eyes up the stairs to where several thin chinks of artificial light filtered through the gaps around the old door. Now that my eyes had grown accustomed to my environment, I could see that it gave off just enough light so we were immersed in a fuzzy grey gloom rather than pitch darkness. "We can't afford to think that way."

I squeezed Wootton's arm and stood, tentatively reaching out, seeking obstacles that might try to trip me. I crept towards the stairs and cocked my head, listening for movement above us.

"I wouldn't," Wootton said softly.

"Wouldn't?"

"Go up there."

He joined me, his arms wrapped around his shoulders. "I've tried that once. Rattled the door. They threw me down the stairs and chucked a bucket of cold water after me."

The hairs on the back of my neck bristled. *Needless cruelty. They wanted Wootton—us—to suffer.*

"Have you heard them mention what their plans are —or were—for you?" I kept my tone casual, not wanting to alert him to my own misgivings.

"They talked about waiting to hear from someone."

"Who? Can you remember a name?"

"Thor, was it? Or Thor Russ? Do you know him?"

"Can't say the name rings a bell." I waited in place, ears and eyes straining, all the time thinking. So, the guys upstairs were waiting to hear from their boss about what to do with Wootton. And now, just to complicate things, me as well. If these were the Bulls that Culpeper was searching for, the ones who tracked down and killed his undercover officers, then I didn't hold out much hope that either of us would make it out of this dank cellar alive.

Not if we waited for them to take all the decisions, anyway.

I had no intention of doing that.

"How far back does this cellar go? Any idea?"

"Quite a way. The wall gives way just to the left of us, and there appears to be a long passage or something. I went a little way in, but"—Wootton laughed nervously — "it's so dark, and I was frightened to go too far." His voice dropped to a whisper. "I heard noises."

"What sort of noises?" I led him back to the wall where we'd been sitting before.

"Echoes. Movement. Things … walking around."

"Rats?" *Ugh*. I wasn't fond of rodents. "We're close to the river here."

"Definitely rats. But something else."

He didn't elucidate any further. I pushed him gently to the floor. "I want you to stay there while I have a little scout around."

"Are you sure you want to do that?" Wootton reached for me. "Maybe I should come with you."

"I want you to stay there and keep an eye and ear out. If you hear anything, or the door starts to open, you call me back, okay?"

"But—"

"It's important, Wootton," I said, squeezing his hand again because the only communication we had in the darkness was touch. I would make better progress without him. After being down here for so long, he was too jumpy. I needed to concentrate.

"Alright."

"Hunch up. Try and stay warm. Don't call out unless you absolutely have to. We don't want to alert them upstairs to what we're doing."

"What *are* we doing?" Wootton asked.

"Getting out of here," I said.

With that, I pulled away from him and carefully shifted sideways along the wall, trailing my hand and shuffling my feet. When the wall ended, I paused and listened.

Almost total silence.

Almost.

I could make out the faint dripping of water. It might be condensation, or it might be water getting in from outside. I shuffled forwards, catching my foot and nearly tripping over something that blocked my path.

Crouching, I waved my hands around the general vicinity, coming into contact with several wooden boxes. I shifted them to one side and inched forward again, following the faint sound of steady dripping. Whatever light there had been alleviating the gloom in the main part of the cellar, it didn't reach this far. When I was happy nothing else was blocking my path, I stood upright and held my arms up, waving them from side to side, stretching my fingertips out and sliding each foot forward, slowly, slowly and then a little faster. At the point of total confidence, I let down my guard and smacked my shoulder on something hard to the left of me.

"Oof." I bounced back and winced.

Reaching up, I examined what I could feel there. Shelving of some kind, stretching from the floor to high above my head. The shelves were packed full of wooden boxes, the same as those I'd tripped over a few moments before. I carefully pulled a box free and, gritting my teeth, attempted to identify the contents within, banishing the thought of spiders and woodlice from my mind. As far as I could tell, this box was full of paper, damp and yet somehow dusty. I shoved it back onto the shelf and wiped my hands on the back of my jeans. There was no point in me searching further without being able to actually see what I was uncovering.

I continued forward, heading for the drip, whatever it was. After what felt like a mile but was probably no more than twenty or thirty feet, I hit a barrier. I lifted my hands once more, tentatively spreading out my palms to feel what was there. I expected cold stone or damp Victorian brickwork, but this was warmer. As I rubbed the surface, it flaked beneath my fingers. Painted wood.

The dripping noise was outside, beyond my reach, but, from here, the sound was as clear as a bell. I inched sideways, still exploring the wood, and felt a slight draught on my face. A slither of a gap in the wood. This was another door? A rear entrance to the basement. What was beyond the door? Another basement? A secret passage somewhere else? The draught on my face suggested otherwise.

I drew close, peered through the crack. I couldn't make out much. It had grown dark, but the sky wasn't black, more a faded deep blue.

It was raining too. The dripping had to be coming from the guttering outside.

Reaching up, I found the edge of the door and the slight chink between it and the frame. Excited now, I ran my fingers all the way around to the right, to the corner and then down until I located the handle, a large iron ring.

Double-checking, I searched every part of the door and frame. There were no bolts. Not on this side. It stood to reason, I suppose, if they wanted to keep people inside the cellar, they would need to lock it from the outside.

Somewhere beyond this door was a way of reaching the outside. And once we were out there, then we could run. We could seek help.

But what if this was a trick? What if someone was waiting for us on the other side? Or perhaps just a lone guard. Either way, we would land ourselves in a whole heap of trouble.

I dismissed those thoughts. They weren't helping. Because what alternative was there?

Nothing ventured, nothing gained.

I wasn't going to wait for anyone else to decide *my* fate. That wasn't how Elise Liddell rolled.

I looped my fingers around the ring and began to turn the handle.

CHAPTER 21

The thick iron ring was cold beneath my fingers. Instinctively, I knew that this would rattle as I tried to turn it. If someone was on guard outside, they would be alerted straight away and that would be it. Game over.

I gently released my grip. I had one chance at this; I couldn't afford to muck it up.

I carefully retraced my steps, sliding my feet along the floor, arms out to the sides, making smoother progress than previously, until the black gave way to grey and I could make out indistinct outlines. I found the edge of the wall and slipped along it. "Wootton," I called softly.

He reached for me, his fingers still icy. I jerked away in shock.

"Come on," I said and pulled him to standing.

"Have you fuh-found a way out?" he asked, his voice sounding loud in the silence.

"Shhh!" I warned him.

"Sorry," he whispered. "Have yuh-you?"

"Maybe. I need you with me." I cast a last look at the door at the top of the wooden stairs. How long before they came back? "Quickly," I urged him, and dragged him behind me.

He stumbled along, not taking the exact same line as me. As we turned into the passage, he kicked one of the boxes I had previously pushed to one side and tripped. I grabbed him as he fell, mis-stepped myself, and we both ended up scrabbling around on the floor.

Beside me, somebody laughed.

I froze.

"Who's there?" I asked.

"Clumsy is as clumsy does." Another laugh, belonging to somebody new, ahead of us.

"Shadow People," Wootton hissed.

I took a deep breath. *Thank the goddess*. Shadow People. That was all. Harmless.

As far as I was aware.

"Are you alright?" I asked him.

"Yeah, just stiff from the cold."

There were giggles up and down the passageway. Just how many of those Shadow People were here? There might have been dozens.

I helped him up again. "Follow me. Stay *right* behind me. Tread where I tread."

"Tread where she treads," a voice ahead of us solemnly repeated.

"Got it." Wootton placed one hand on the small of my back. "Let's go, Grandma."

"Watch it," I said, but his gentle jibe gave me a lift. He didn't sound so defeated.

Tentatively, I moved forwards. Once we'd cleared the hurdle of the boxes, with the exception of the shelving to my left—and now, of course, I knew what to watch out for—we were almost home free. Step by step, we moved in unison until we reached the wooden door.

I pulled him into a crouch beside me and put my lips to his ear. "There's a door here. It's probably bolted on the outside. Maybe padlocked. I have no idea. I didn't want to try it out until you were here."

"What if there's someone out there?"

"There may well be. But we have to try *something*, Wootton."

"Maybe this Thor will tell them to let us go. Perhaps we should wait. Not make them angry by attempting an escape?"

Images of the men I had found dead in Packhorse Close invaded my memory. *No.* If these were the Labyrinthians, they had no intention of letting us live. Not knowing we were somehow mixed up with the Dark Squad.

"I want to give this a go, Wootton," I told him, keeping my voice gentle. He was so young, so naïve to the evil in the world, and that despite having lived in Tumble Town since birth. "Are you with me?"

He faltered for a moment, then I felt his hair brush against my cheek. He was nodding. "Yes. I'm with you."

I pulled him to his feet again then gently searched for the iron ring. Once more I looped my fingers through it and, in painful increments, I began to turn it, waiting for the loud scraping clink and clunk sounds that iron on iron makes.

It clicked.

I held my breath.

No other noise from behind the door.

I turned the ring another half inch.

It clinked.

I waited.

And again.

This time I turned the ring as far as it would go. If all was right, the latch would be suspended in mid-air. All I needed to do now was push.

I did so. The door gave slightly but didn't open.

"Rats!" I hissed, not that I wasn't prepared for this particular obstacle.

"Where?" Wootton jumped.

"Not that sort of rats. The door. It *is* bolted. I was afraid it might be."

"What now?" I could hear the panic in Wootton's breathing.

"It'll be fine," I soothed. "Locks and bolts are all in a day's work for the MOWPD." I lifted my hand and ran it around the top right edge of the door, sensing the layout beyond. "*Quiescis*," I whispered. "*Resigno*."

The bolt drew back as though it had been bathed in a vat of baby oil. As silent and smooth as you like.

I repeated the process at the bottom.

"That's it." I breathed out in a rush. "And now the handle again."

From behind us, back in the main part of the cellar, we heard a crash.

"Time to go," whispered a voice next to me. A Shadow Person, breathing down my neck.

"Agreed," I told it.

I twisted the ring and pushed. The door stuck.

"Someone's coming, Elise!" Wootton's cold hand against my back was firm, as though by pushing me the door would miraculously open.

"Hurry, hurry," came another voice.

I grabbed the ring in both hands and twisted it, throwing my weight against the door at the same time. The wooden door, slightly warped from the damp, gave way and I burst out into the evening air, Wootton at my heels. The momentum forced me forwards and, for a heart-stopping moment, I seemed to beat at the air, then Wootton grabbed a hold of my t-shirt and dragged me to safety. We were on a towpath, a canal fed by water from the Thames eight to ten feet below us.

"Holy macaroni!" My knees turned to jelly.

"Elise! We need to get going, they must have heard us."

Wootton was right. I hurriedly scanned our surroundings, my brain working overtime. Gas lamps sporadically lit the way, casting deep shadows where the light did not reach. I'd lost my bearings and wasn't sure which was north or south. But did it really matter? We needed to find somewhere populated, somewhere where the Bulls would not dare to attack us.

Behind us, I heard the noise of wooden boxes tumbling. Perhaps one of our pursuers had collided with the shelving unit. They were close behind.

I yanked Wootton's arm and ran, leading him to the

left. We clattered down the towpath, splashing through puddles, avoiding barrels and fishing equipment left out overnight. My eyes flitted this way and that, searching for a potential hiding place or a turning that would flummox our assailants.

Up ahead, a bridge loomed out of the darkness and I raced up the steps and across it, turning my head to check on our progress. There were three men following us, rough, rugged types—not the Viking nor anyone else I recognised. They weren't gaining ground on us that I could see; fortunately, Wootton was as fit as a fiddle, although a little weak from his time in captivity, and all my running was standing me in good stead. These were desperate times. We *had* to get away.

We jumped down the steps at the other side and instinctively ran right. I couldn't see for sure, but it looked as though our progress to the left would have been thwarted by a large warehouse jutting out above the canal itself.

"Keep on!" I heard the call of our pursuers behind me. "We've got them now."

*What did that mean?*

We slid between two buildings, running at full pelt down a narrow ginnel that grew ever narrower and sheltered us from the rain. Now I could hear the sound of flowing water, the Thames, somewhere ahead of us, the tinny chink of spinnakers from boats moored close by, but tantalisingly the river lay out of reach. The ginnel was coming to an end, another warehouse blocking our way. I skidded to a halt, Wootton running into the back of me. Breathlessly I pointed at the barrier ahead. "We're trapped!"

"This way!" He grabbed my arm, and I followed him into the narrowest space between two ramshackle sheds. He went first, as skinny as a rake. I followed a little more slowly, my chest painfully compressed.

*Please don't let me get trapped here*, I prayed. What a way to go, murdered while jammed between two stinking fish warehouses.

"Where did they go?" The voice, so close, sounded genuinely perplexed. It was met with a giggle from one of the Shadow People.

"Please don't give us away," I whispered, mostly to myself, but they must have heard us.

"Where did they go?" the voice repeated with mock solemnity.

"They slipped away," a second voice answered.

"Away, away!" The whispers were taken up by others. Dozens of them. All around us.

I continued to slide after Wootton, snagging my t-shirt on a nail. I wrenched it free and tumbled out into a larger space, a boatyard of sorts, small rowing boats and fishermen's paraphernalia all over the place. In my hurry to get away from our pursuers, I collided with a faded pink fishing buoy. It clattered as it rolled over.

One of the men shone a torch through the gap from the other side. Wootton and I stood together, a pair of rabbits in the headlights.

"There they are!" The man with the torch tried to follow us through the narrow gap, but his wider bulk prevented him from doing so.

"Go round!" he yelled. "Cut them off!"

The light from the torch disappeared.

"There's only one other way out of here," Wootton said, pointing to a passageway between two buildings.

"If we go that way, we're going to run slap-bang into them," I said.

"Then what? We don't have much time!"

"We hide!" My head swivelled from left to right. I pivoted three hundred and sixty degrees. So many hiding places, most of them absurdly obvious.

It had to be something that looked like it wouldn't be worth hiding in, something slightly open to the elements—

I spotted a tugboat, approximately fourteen feet in length. It had been tipped upside down, the front hoisted partially into the air, jacked up on wooden beams so it could receive attention from below. Most of its weight rested on one side—I couldn't tell you whether it was port or starboard, but you get the picture. "There!"

"*What?*" Wootton protested.

"The wheelhouse!" I grabbed his arm and dragged him over; I could already see light playing on the walls of the warehouse directly opposite the passageway. The man with the torch was coming straight for us.

"We've run out of time and options," I said, and pushed him underneath the boat. He crawled towards the rear, where the small wheelhouse was, on his hands and knees, and I followed him. We couldn't both get inside. "Scrunch up," I told him. "Make yourself as small as possible." He did as I said, as bendy as plasticine. I manoeuvred myself into the space directly behind him, nestling among the shadows, and pulled my knees to my chest, wrapping my arms around them.

"Keep quiet and don't move a muscle," I whispered to Wootton. It hardly needed saying. He wasn't going to willingly give us away, was he? "But remember to breathe."

Rather than hold my breath, I made a conscious effort to calm it. Holding your breath inevitably leads to taking in big gulps of air, and that's when you make a noise. Far better to calm yourself and take shallower in-breaths.

Yellow light played along the periphery of my vision. The men were arriving in the yard.

"Come out, come out, wherever you are," one of them sang, and giggled. That melodic laugh was probably the single most unnerving sound I'd ever heard. My guts twisted. How easy it is for some people to contemplate harming another and make light of it.

I edged my head sideways, peering out from behind the wheelhouse, hoping to get a glimpse of the pursuers. I had every intention of getting out of this situation in one piece, and when I did, I wanted to be able to identify these men and ensure they were sent down for a long, long time.

Still only three of them. Two with torches, one without. Occasionally one would move into view while illuminated by another's torch. The first guy was chunky, rounded belly and face, dark floppy hair and rough beard, wearing a striped jumper. The second was taller, muscular, blond with a strange topknot, with tattoos on every available stretch of skin bar his face. The third, the one who barked the most orders, seemed the most disagreeable of all. He had a shaven scalp, his head appearing too small for his broad shoulders. His eyes were glittering black diamonds. He moved with aggression, shoulders rolling, arms slack, the way a panther stalks its prey. I wouldn't have wanted a straight fight with him under any circumstances.

He joined his friends in the centre of the yard.

"They must have managed to squeeze past us," Stripy Man said.

"They didn't," the Panther growled. "They're here somewhere." He lifted his nose and sniffed. "I can smell them."

Wootton caught his breath. A tiny sound. So faint even I struggled to hear it—and I was sitting inches from him. There was no way it could have travelled. Yet the Panther's head pivoted in our direction.

*What dark magick could this be?*

"Turn the place upside down and find them. And bring them to me. The longer it takes, the more furious I will be, and the slower and more painful the consequences."

I might have been wrong, but from the angle of his head and the glint in his eyes, I imagined at that moment he was addressing me and Wootton directly.

The rain drummed on the bottom of the boat above my head. Stripy Man and Topknot Man had made a jolly good show of searching everywhere and everything. They had upended barrels, unravelled fishing nets, kicked piles of rubbish around, rattled the locked doors of the warehouses and peered through the dark windows of inaccessible sheds. Stripy Man had even, at one stage, shone his torch underneath the boat and swung it around. He wouldn't have seen Wootton unless he'd actually slid under the hull and joined us, but I was amazed he didn't notice my boots, shining under the glare of the concentrated light, despite the amount of mud caked on them.

After twenty-five minutes of exhaustive searching, they had nothing, and Stripy Man had started to whine. "It's a waste of time. I'm telling you, Boss, they escaped the yard before we made it round here."

*Boss, eh?* I made a mental note of that information. Was this the man Culpeper was looking for?

"We'd be better off combing the lanes," Topknot Man agreed.

"If they made it into the lanes, there wouldn't be any point looking for them." The Boss's voice was soft. "They'd be home free. No, they're here somewhere."

Stripy Man sighed loudly, like a petulant kid. "Come on! It's a wild goose—"

The next moment he hit the dirt, face down.

I jumped.

There had been no warning. The Boss had felled him without saying a word. I waited for Stripy Man to move, for some indication that he was still alive and would stand up at any second, blustering and whining and apologising.

But he didn't do any of that.

A shiver raced down my spine. This Boss guy, the Panther, wasn't messing.

"Do I have to send for reinforcements?" he was asking, in the same gentle tone he'd been using previously. He wasn't even the slightest bit ruffled.

"No, sir!" Topknot Man wasn't about to make the same mistake as his colleague. "Absolutely not."

"Burn it."

"What?" Topknot Man glanced around. "Burn …?"

"Burn it all. Everything in the yard. The warehouses. Everything. We'll either smoke them out or turn them to ashes. Either way, it's their funeral."

"Yes, sir."

"You'll find petrol in my lock-up."

"Yes, sir," Topknot Man repeated, and I watched as he took to his heels and disappeared from my view. The sound of his running footsteps faded as he raced down the passage away from the boatyard.

How long did that give us? How far did he have to go?

*What to do? What to do?*

Stripy Man had not moved a muscle. I could only conclude he was dead. That meant Wootton and I were left alone here, with only the Boss. It would be two against one.

But Wootton was no fighter, and the Boss had already proven his magick skills. They were equal to mine, perhaps superior. But it would be our best— possibly our only—chance to escape. I reached a hand through the door of the wheelhouse to alert Wootton to my intention.

Somewhere a phone rang. Not mine. Not Wootton's.

Not the Boss's either. As I watched, he approached Stripy Man's prone body and knelt beside him. I could clearly see his face now. It was angular: square jaw, sharp cheekbones. A thin mouth. Only his nose was slightly kinked and therefore lacking symmetry.

He rummaged in Stripy Man's trouser pocket and extracted the phone, took one look at the display and frowned. Nonetheless, he thumbed the screen and lifted it to his ear. "Sir?"

Someone higher than the Boss. Who was the Boss's boss? Thor? Imagine what Culpeper and the Dark Squad could do with such a phone. The traces they could make, the numbers it would yield.

"He's indisposed, sir," the Panther was saying.

I wanted that phone.

"I'm taking care of a little problem."

*Needed* it.

"That's what we thought you'd say. It's in hand."

I stared greedily at the device in the Boss's hand.

"And the woman?"

I refocused. They were discussing me and Wootton.

"Quite right, sir." The Boss chuckled. "Eminently disposable. Consider it done."

That sounded pretty final to me.

I shifted slightly, but Wootton's hand shot out from the wheelhouse and grabbed my arm.

"Don't!" he hissed.

I heard footsteps running towards us, gravel

crunching beneath feet, the sloshing of liquid in an iron can.

"Thank you, sir. Goodbye."

"I have it, Boss!" Topknot Man was back.

We were out of time.

"Let's get to work," the Boss said. "And keep an eye out for any rats deserting sinking ships."

# CHAPTER 22

I was in a quandary.

I could only assume that Topknot Man might be the easier to contain, which meant I should go after the Boss first. But the second I wriggled out of my hiding space, he would see me—and that would be the end of the confrontation, I imagined.

I strongly suspected he knew exactly where we were. He'd never moved from his position since he'd arrived in the boatyard. Entirely unphased by the relentless rain, he'd paced the same square of space, rarely angling his body any way but toward us. *Why was he toying with us?*

If only there was a way to distract him and draw his attention elsewhere.

Topknot Man had moved out of sight, but I listened to the swoosh of liquid in the can and the spattering as it spilled on the ground.

"That'll do," the Boss called. "The wood in those

buildings is rotten. They'll burn like matchsticks despite the weather. Here"—he directed Topknot Man—"burn the boats."

Wootton groaned softly. "We have to get out."

I stilled him with a touch, waiting for a moment that might never come. Above our heads, liquid splashed the side of the boat and pooled on the ground just feet away. The foul odour of petrol reached me almost immediately. I recoiled from the stench.

A light flashed, and the building opposite us, behind the Boss, blazed immediately yellow. Flames leapt towards the sky. Within seconds, all the warehouses I could see were engulfed. Rivulets, little fingers of orange fire, ran towards us in slow motion and I was reminded of those cartoons where some poor animal tries to blow out the flame before it reaches the gunpowder.

It was now or never.

"Follow me," I told Wootton. "And once you're out, you run for your life!"

I shifted to one side, ignoring the pain from my cramped limbs, and rolled onto my side. Without my wand, my magick would not be the most accurate—but hopefully it would be enough. I now had a better view of the boatyard. The warehouses to the far right were not yet aflame.

I pointed at an oil barrel. "*Pervolito!*" I hissed, mustering as much intent into that single word as possible. The barrel flew upwards and thumped against the nearest warehouse.

The Boss turned to look.

That was all the distraction I needed. I rolled again, through a malodorous oily puddle and onto my knees. I aimed the flat of my palm at the Boss, even as he turned back to me, his attention caught by my movement. "*Laedo!*" I shouted.

It was a spell I'd often used on suspects who were running away from me. By rights, with the amount of intent I'd mustered, I should have knee-capped the Boss. I fully expected him to fall to the floor. But he barely swayed.

Now, forewarned, his hands were up, his eyes glowing with a red as savage as the fires burning behind him.

With a whoosh, the tug boat lit up. I felt the heat of the flames. The sudden rush of air. I couldn't turn around, couldn't check on Wootton's progress. I couldn't take my eyes from the Boss.

"Give it up," he said to me.

We faced each other, like some stand-off from a Wild West movie, the world around us an inferno of insanity. The stench of burning wood and rubber and electrics, cloying and sticky, permeated the air and coated my lungs with a greasy residue.

I had no choice.

I had to try and disarm him.

I had to cast an injury hex.

"*Damage!*" I roared and threw my energy with all my might.

He was more than a match for me. With one soft movement, he was able to deflect my magick effortlessly and send it straight back to me, just as I'd feared. The wave slammed into me, and I fell, incapacitated, the way someone might had they been tasered.

I lay in the rank puddle, winded, fire roaring all around, its tendrils of death reaching for me, Wootton nowhere to be seen. *Please let him get away*, I begged. *Let him be safe*.

*Please!*

But even as I cast that thought out into the ether, Topknot Man reappeared, driving Wootton forward, his huge hand around my poor office junior's neck, his fingers almost touching at the throat. I remembered the men I'd found, dead in doorways. *This* was their killer!

The Boss advanced on us, a grim sneer on his cruel lips, his hands outstretched.

Still half-paralysed from the hex, I twisted onto my side, desperate to get away, to find a means to save us both. I scrabbled at the ground, my nails breaking in my frantic attempt to claw some distance between me and the Boss. The heat from the boat was burning my face, drying my tears. Turning fully onto my front, I prepared to slide like a snake if I had to, waiting for an explosion of pain as the Boss ended my life …

Something white bobbed into my peripheral vision. I blinked the acrid tears from my eyes, trying to focus …

Ahead of me, staring straight back my way, were chocolate eyes, both stern and strong.

A white rabbit.

Not, after all, a harbinger of death … but a beacon of hope.

A chance of survival.

After that, everything happened instantaneously. Shapes emerged out of the shadows, and beams of energy lit up the boatyard like trace fire.

"On the ground, now!" someone yelled, and Wootton, regardless of whether they were shouting at him or not, freed himself from Topknot's clutches and flung himself onto the ground beside me, wrapping an arm around my back as though he would protect me.

"Who are these people?" he asked, his eyes full of fear.

"The Dark Squad," I told him. "Otherwise known as the cavalry."

"On the ground! I won't tell you again!"

There must have been eight members of the Dark Squad, maybe more. All of them were dressed in dark clothes, several of them wearing robes with the hoods pulled down over their eyes, eager to remain incognito. Each of them had a wand drawn, and by the tense yet alert way they moved, I could only guess they were prepared to use ultimate force.

I risked a glance over my shoulder, a spasm of pain shooting up my right-hand side. The Boss was standing alone, his hands palms out. Had this been my shout, I wouldn't have understood his intentions. Did the hands mean, 'Okay, I'm backing down'? He'd made no move to kneel. Or did they signify his readiness to fire more injurious magick towards the Dark Squad's officers?

My fear was the Dark Squad would construe it as

the latter and obliterate the Boss without a second thought. There'd be nothing of him left. Not a thread of clothing, not a fingernail, not a single hair particle.

I knew that's what this man would prefer. He would take his secrets with him rather than give up the Labyrinthians.

"The phone," I tried to call, but my voice was lost, small among the roaring crackle of flames and the chorus of shouted commands.

"What?" Wootton had heard me.

"We have to get the phone," I croaked. "We can't let them kill him."

"On the ground!" Topknot was clearly not playing ball either. Wootton and I turned to watch as he lurched at an officer drawing closer to him, his huge hands like paddles. I thought of the lives of the Dark Squad under-cover operatives, of those he had crushed. He wouldn't hesitate to do the same again.

He almost caught the officer nearest him, but a flash of electric energy and Topknot withered like a piece of dry paper and began to crumple to the floor. By the time his body hit the ground, there was nothing of him but ash.

"No!" I struggled to sit up, but my right-hand side wasn't willing to do my bidding.

"Wait," Wootton said and jumped up. I reached for him. Far too slow. I narrowly missed his hand as he took off. He was running, not away from danger, as I would have preferred him to do, but towards it.

Towards the Boss, in fact.

"Wootton!" I shrieked in terror. What was he doing?

The Dark Squad were converging on the Boss. He had raised his hands higher, palms out. I knew what that signified. He was intending to take them all on. It would weaken his attack to scatter his magick in such a way, but that didn't matter to him. I'd seen this behaviour before. He was hell-bent on self-destruction, and he would take as many of them with him as he could.

As the Dark Squad trained their magick in his direction and prepared to fire, as the Boss lifted his head to the skies and smiled, drawing his power from the universe, Wootton flew at him, hitting his target square and low. A glorious rugby tackle by someone who would have been lucky to make fly half on his school's B team. The momentum knocked the Boss off balance, his arms flailed, his magick spun harmlessly awry.

Instantaneously, most of the Dark Squad officers pulled their own attacks. One or two, slightly slower on the uptake, fired but managed to misdirect their magick at the last possible instant. Only one fired on his target. Wootton and the Boss landed on the wet ground together, the Boss howling with pain, holding one arm up in front of his face, a bloodied stump, the hand gone.

Wootton rolled with him and leapt to his feet. For good measure, he kicked the Boss hard where it would hurt the most. As the Boss curled over, cradling both arm and groin, Wootton ransacked his pockets, patting him down until he found what he was looking for.

Finally he jerked upright, panting, a huge beam

painted across his face. He triumphantly brandished the phone aloft.

"Mission accomplished, Grandma," he shouted. "Mission accomplished!"

CHAPTER 23

I groaned as a faceless member of the Dark Squad
carefully pulled me to my feet. He supported me
by holding onto my right elbow as I limped, with
difficulty, towards Minsk, Wootton scurrying along in
my wake, holding out the phone. Rain beat relentlessly
down on our heads. I was almost glad of it. There was
something life-affirming about its cool freshness. It
would go some way to help douse the flames.

The Boss was still creating a fuss about the loss of
his hand—perhaps understandably—but several
members of Minsk's team were preparing to spirit him
away, and someone was wrapping a huge bandage
around his stump.

"How are you doing?" Minsk asked as we neared her.
She seemed entirely unflustered by the events of the last
few minutes, sitting atop an upended rowing boat, her
eyes darting around, keenly appraising all that was
going on.

"I'll live," I said. "I've never been on the receiving end

of one of my own hexes before, so that'll teach me." I tried to laugh, but that sent a sharp pain radiating out from my solar plexus and caused my chest muscles to spasm. I wrapped my left arm around myself.

"I can arrange for a doctor," Minsk said, "but my team can't hang around. I'm sure you understand."

I thought she meant all of us would have to leave, but clearly she didn't. She nodded at the masked figure holding my arm. He relinquished his grasp and loped off to join his colleagues.

"Thanks for all your help," Minsk added as she turned after him and prepared to hop off the boat.

"Wait," I called. "That's it?"

She stopped. "That's it." Her warm eyes gave nothing away; her whiskers didn't so much as twitch. "As your young assistant said, mission accomplished. Thanks to you, we've a body to identify and a prisoner to interrogate. It's a job well done."

"Do you have any idea who they are?" I asked.

"Not a clue as of yet, but we'll work on it. The body has the tattoo, so that's a start."

"There's this as well." I beckoned to Wootton and he joined us, holding out the phone. "Your man over there with the missing hand? He took it out of the dead guy's pocket. He spoke into it, and he called the person he talked to 'boss.'"

"Excellent!" Minsk twitched an ear at one of her team and someone came forward to take the phone from Wootton. Minsk cocked her head and stared at my young office assistant. "We'll have our digital forensics team take a look at that. I'm sure it will spawn a great deal of information." She nodded. "It was brave of you to dive in that way. If we'd had to obliterate him, he would have taken that information with him."

Wootton's face was grave. "That's what Elise said. I figured if she was risking her life, I needed to help her out."

"You make a good team."

I reached out and hugged Wootton. He flushed with pleasure at Minsk's words.

"The other man," I said, "the one with the Topknot. Did you see the size of his hands?"

"I did. Sadly, there's no body for us to look at, but one of my team has recorded everything. We'll take a close look at his image."

I pointed at Wootton's neck. "He had his hand wrapped around Wootton and the fingers almost met in the middle. I'm thinking he was the one responsible for the latest batch of deaths of undercover officers, although presumably not the historical ones."

Wootton did a double take. "You what?"

"All those dates you found," I quickly explained, "they related to the deaths of undercover officers."

Minsk narrowed her eyes. "You need to keep that a secret," she told him.

"I will," Wootton stammered, "I promise."

"I might send someone to take photos of any bruises you have on your neck, if you don't mind."

"Of course. Whatever you need." Wootton gingerly rubbed at his throat, possibly imagining what might have happened to him.

"If you need fingerprints"—I pointed at a petrol can lying on its side—"he was carrying that."

"Good stuff. We'll grab that before we go." In the distance we could hear the wail of sirens. Maybe fire engines, maybe MOWPD. Time was running out. Minsk and her team needed to make a quick getaway.

*Now.*

"What about the tattooist?" I asked hurriedly. "Did you manage to pick him up?"

"We traced your call to Tetris Alley and found the remnants of the phone we gave you. We have officers searching the surrounding buildings and shops."

He'd have done a runner by now. "The man I spoke to looked a little like a Viking. Tall, well-built. Hair down here." I gestured at my waist. "The tattoo parlour was called Wasted Youth Tattoos."

"My men are on it," Minsk replied, her tone reassuring. I could tell she was itching to get back to work, maybe start interrogating her prisoner. If I kept her any longer, he'd bleed out before she could do so.

I nodded. "Of course. I'm not suggesting you don't know what you're doing."

I hooked an arm around Wootton. Anyone might have imagined I was just being friendly, but really, I needed his strength to keep me upright. The whole of my right-hand side was throbbing.

"You should see a doctor," Minsk reaffirmed. "I can call one out for you, if you like?"

I waved the offer away. "I'll be fine, honestly."

"Alright."

I edged away, and, with Wootton taking my weight, hobbled for the exit to the boatyard.

"Elise?" she called after me.

I paused.

"You did good."

I smiled and squeezed Wootton's arm. He led me away. Where the passageway began, I leaned against the wall for a moment to catch my breath. With difficulty, I turned my head to take one final look at the scene of devastation behind us, the burning warehouses and boats.

The sky was glowing orange, the air thick with black smoke and alive with the crackle of flames.

But of the Dark Squad, of Minsk, of the Panther and the body of Stripy Man?

There was no sign.

# EPILOGUE

Forty-eight hours later, I was slumped over my desk, nursing a headache and a glass of Blue Goblin.

That is to say, I had a small shot glass in my hand, full of potent liquor, but I wasn't drinking it, just inhaling it.

Half of my body ached. I'd taken copious amounts of painkillers over the past couple of days in an effort to alleviate the worst of it, but still felt as though I had sprained every single muscle on one side. Truth to tell, I was impressed my magick had turned out to be as potent as it was.

I was alone. Wootton was taking a few days off to recover; Snitch was out and about, doing whatever Snitch did when he wasn't hanging out at Wonderland, and I had no idea where Ezra was.

I could have done with an early night, but I wasn't entirely convinced I could find the strength to walk home. I wished, for once, that I could summon a taxi to

JEANNIE WYCHERLEY

take me, but taxis weren't a thing in Tumble Town. Unless you fancied riding on the back of a mule.

Sighing, I returned my attention to my computer screen and read back what I'd written. I'd been updating my Dodo files. Had we gone as far as we could with the Kevin Makepeace investigation? What other avenues could I pursue?

A soft scratching at the door alerted me to company. I glanced up but couldn't see anyone. Leaning sideways, I caught a flash of white. In the shake of a lamb's tail—or a rabbit's, in this case—Minsk had jumped onto the chair opposite my desk.

"DC Minsk!" I raised my eyebrows. "It's a pleasure to see you again." I'd been thinking about her a lot—how well she had controlled the situation at the boatyard, the gravity with which she approached her work. I liked that about her. I'd have valued a colleague like her.

"You too, DI Liddell." Her whiskers twitched. "Is that Blue Goblin vodka?"

"It is." Unsure, I held the glass out to her, then placed it on the edge of the desk. She hopped neatly up and took a sip, waggled her ears and winced.

"That's so bad, it's good," she said, with a definite air of satisfaction.

"Help yourself," I said.

She took another sip. "I really shouldn't. Have you ever seen a drunk rabbit?"

"I haven't," I smiled, "but I bet it's fun."

"I'm the life and soul of any party. You should see my twerk. It's the cutest."

"I can believe that." I giggled. "I'd pay good money to see it!"

We were silent for a moment. She took another sip of the vodka. I waited, certain she would get to the point of her visit in her own time.

Eventually, she sat back on her haunches and fixed me with her mesmerising eyes. "It probably won't surprise you to learn that, so far, our mutual friend isn't saying much."

She was right. It didn't surprise me in the least. He'd been prepared to die rather than be taken alive.

"We're still in the process of unlocking the information in the phone, but we *have* found some communication that"—she hesitated—"interests us."

I nodded. She was being understandably scant with the details. I wouldn't have expected anything else.

She lowered her voice. "But I came here this evening because I wanted to tell you that we are almost certain —as certain as we can be—that the perpetrator of the murders of the undercover officers over the past few years was indeed the third man at the scene."

Topknot Man. It made me shiver to think how close Wootton had come to obliteration at that brute's hands.

"You can draw a line under that, then," I said, pleased for her.

"For now. Given the size and scale of the Labyrinthians, there will always be others willing to take his place —we can be certain of that."

I nodded. Policing was a grim business. "Thank you for coming over here and letting me know."

"It was the least I could do." She licked out the dregs

of vodka from the glass, then hopped down from the desk to the chair and from there to the floor.

I pushed my seat back, intending to see her out.

She stared up at me as I limped out from behind my desk. "I know nothing I've said helps your case, and I'm sorry about that, Elise."

I met her eyes. Was she trying to tell me that my case wasn't her case? She'd told me so before. I shrugged.

"However … there is an alignment." She was choosing her words carefully. "One of the text messages on the phone …"

"Go on," I said, my heart beating a little faster.

"Was a response to someone enquiring about a 'KM'."

"DC Makepeace?"

"We think so. The message was sent a few days before you found his body."

He'd been dead a few days when I stumbled across him. It could be a coincidence though, I told myself.

"We traced the number that made the enquiry and unfortunately, that mobile is now defunct."

"Okay." I guarded my tone.

"But it shows up in MOWPD files in a recent investigation into the *second* murder in Packhorse Close. It was the contact number given by the gentleman you apprehended at the scene."

"Mr Tweedle?"

"Yes."

The word dropped like a stone in the quiet atmosphere of the office.

"What was the response?" I had to know.

Minsk's spine was rigid. "Kill him."

"Whoa." I swallowed.

This evidence suggested that there was some link between Mr Tweedle and the Labyrinthians. The Labyrinth Society had known about DC Makepeace, and they had wanted him killed.

And this Mr Tweedle?

I'd had him! And I'd let him get away!

It was a kick in the teeth.

"I thought you should know," Minsk continued softly. "In case you were thinking of closing the case."

I glanced back at the desk where Dodo had been murdered. Monkton, bless him, thought he had Cerys Pritchard bang to rights, and with her accomplice dead, to his way of thinking, justice had been served. But in my opinion, we'd only just scratched the surface.

"It's a long way from being closed," I replied firmly.

Minsk pushed the door closed. I'd imagined she was on her way out, so I was surprised when she hopped back towards me. "I was hoping you'd say that," she said.

"You were?"

"I think we should pool resources."

"You're not going to order me back undercover, are you?" I asked distrustfully. The piercings had gone, but I was still waiting for the tattoo inks to wash off my arms. Naked, I looked like a really bad watercolour painting that had been left out in the rain.

"*I'm* not going to order you to do anything," she said. "*We'll* be partners. We'll discuss all aspects of the case and make joint decisions. You liaise with your branch of MOWPD and me with mine. What do you think?"

Taken aback, I collapsed into my chair. Minsk jumped back up to the desk. She was right. The Dodo case was wide open. The Labyrinthian investigation a complete mess. Working together, we might just be able to make some inroads.

"Let's do it," I said.

"Excellent!" Minsk lifted a paw to high-five me, then spun the shot glass my way, her meaning clear. "I'll drink to that!"

"I thought you said you shouldn't?" I reached for the bottle I kept in the desk drawer.

She smirked. "I thought you'd pay good money to see a bunny twerk?"

"Do I have to pay even if we're partners?" I asked.

"You make a valid point! Partners watch for free," Minsk agreed, and raised her glass. "Here's to the start of a beautiful friendship!"

# CURIOUS ABOUT WHAT HAPPENS NEXT?

**_Tweedledumb and Tweedledie: Wonderland Detective Agency Book 3_**

In Tumble Town, the shadows know your name …
And, as ex-detective Elise Riddell knows only too well,
that's not necessarily a good thing.
Wizard Dodo is dead.
And so is DC Makepeace.
The common thread that links them is Cerys Pritchard,
incarcerated in an institution for the criminally insane.
She's not talking. Not in any way that makes sense.
Then there's the ultra secret Labyrinthine Society.
They're determined to see Elise dead.
She's equally determined to stay alive.
She also wants to bring Dodo's killers to justice.
Game on!
Find _Tweedledumb and Tweedledie_ on Amazon.

# HAVE YOU ENJOYED THE RABBIT HOLE MURDERS?

Please leave a review
Have you enjoyed *The Rabbit Hole Murders*?
Please leave me a review on Amazon or Goodreads.
Reviews help spread the word about my work, which is
great for me because I find new readers!
And why not join my mailing list to find out more
about what I'm up to and what is coming out next? Just
pop along to my website and fill in the quick form.
You'll find me at jeanniewycherley.co.uk
If you'd like to join my closed author group you'll find it
here at
https://www.facebook.com/
groups/JeannieWycherleysFiends/
Please let me know you've reviewed one of my books
when you apply.

ALSO BY JEANNIE WYCHERLEY

**The Complete Wonky Inn Series (in chronological reading order)**
The Wonkiest Witch: Wonky Inn Book 1
The Ghosts of Wonky Inn: Wonky Inn Book 2
Weird Wedding at Wonky Inn: Wonky Inn Book 3
The Witch Who Killed Christmas: Wonky Inn Christmas Special
Fearful Fortunes and Terrible Tarot: Wonky Inn Book 4
The Mystery of the Marsh Malaise: Wonky Inn Book 5
The Mysterious Mr Wylie: Wonky Inn Book 6
The Great Witchy Cake Off: Wonky Inn Book 7
Vengeful Vampire at Wonky Inn: Wonky Inn Book 8
Witching in a Winter Wonkyland: A Wonky Inn Christmas Cozy Special
A Gaggle of Ghastly Grandmamas: Wonky Inn Book 9
Magic, Murder and a Movie Star: Wonky Inn Book 10
O' Witchy Town of Whittlecombe: A Wonky Inn Christmas Cozy Special

Judge, Jury and Jailhouse Rockcakes: Wonky Inn Book 11

A Midsummer Night's Wonky: Wonky Inn Book 12

**Spellbound Hound**

Ain't Nothing but a Pound Dog: Spellbound Hound Magic and Mystery Book 1

A Curse, a Coven and a Canine: Spellbound Hound Magic and Mystery Book 2

Bark Side of the Moon: Spellbound Hound Magic and Mystery Book 3

Master of Puppies: Spellbound Hound Magic and Mystery Book 4 (TBC)

**Wonderland Detective Agency**

Dead as a Dodo: Wonderland Detective Agency Book 1

The Rabbit Hole Murders: Wonderland Detective Agency Book 2

Tweedledumb and Tweedledie: Wonderland Detective Agency Book 3 (Coming August 2021)

The Curious Incident at the Pig and Pepper: Wonderland Detective Agency Book 4 (TBC)

The Municipality of Lost Souls (2020)

Midnight Garden: The Extra Ordinary World Novella Series Book 1 (2019)

Beyond the Veil (2018) http://mybook.to/BTV

Crone (2017) http://mybook.to/CroneJW

ALSO BY JEANNIE WYCHERLEY

A Concerto for the Dead and Dying (short story, 2018)
http://mybook.to/ConcertoDead
Deadly Encounters: A collection of short stories (2017)
http://mybook.to/DeadlyEncounters
Keepers of the Flame: A love story (Novella, 2018)
http://mybook.to/keepers

**Non-Fiction**
Losing my best Friend: Thoughtful support for those
affected by dog bereavement or pet loss (2017) http://
mybook.to/LosingMyBestFriend

**Follow Jeannie Wycherley**
Find out more at on the website https://www.
jeanniewycherley.co.uk/
You can tweet Jeannie https://
twitter.com/Thecushionlady
Or visit her on Facebook for her fiction https://www.
facebook.com/jeanniewycherley/
Follow Jeannie on Instagram (for bears and books)
https://www.instagram.com/jeanniewycherley/
Sign up for Jeannie's newsletter on her website

OUT NOW

*The Creature from the Grim Mire*
There's no chance of a quiet life when you've aliens in your attic.
Felicity Westmacott craves solitude.
But something with a hearty appetite is stalking the moor and terrifying the locals.
And things going bump in the night puts paid to her equilibrium.
As does the mysterious appearance of an elderly gentleman.
He claims to be a time traveller.
Obviously as nutty as a fruitcake, he wants her to run a creche.
For baby aliens.
Now her secret's out and other people are interested in Felicity's unusual house guests.
Her 'children' are in terrible danger.
Will Felicity save her young charges? Or will she finish her novel instead?

Find out in *The Creature from the Grim Mire*.

If you've ever wondered what HG Wells got up to in his spare time, you'll love this alien invasion tale set on Dartmoor in South Devon, UK. This is the perfect light-hearted read for lovers of humorous sci-fi mysteries or cozy animal mysteries, or indeed anyone seeking a bit of fun escapism with a cup of tea and a slice of cake. But keep an eye on your snacks – there are hungry aliens loose. Some of them can eat their body weight in Custard Creams!

*The Creature from the Grim Mire* is a collaboration between father and daughter, Peter Alderson Sharp (*The Sword, the Wolf and the Rock*) and Jeannie Wycherley (the Wonky Inn books, *Crone, The Municipality of Lost Souls* etc.).

*The Municipality of Lost Souls*
Vengeful souls don't stay dead
They taunt the minds of the living until they throw themselves from clifftops.
Yet death turns a profit when you drive ships onto rocks to plunder riches.
Agatha knows one thing for sure: respect the dead.
Especially those who did not die quietly.
Now, a lonely witch has conjured a young sailor's soul.
And woken them all.

Only Agatha knows the truth.
She hears it in the whispers drifting across the waves.
She hears it in the crackle of the flames.
And the marauders will stop at nothing to silence her.
Shh … Listen …
The Dead Are Coming …

From the Amazon bestselling author of Crone comes a thoroughly original and spellbinding piece of storytelling. *The Municipality of Lost Souls* is a gothic ghost story set in 1860s England with characters destined to haunt you forever.
For readers of dark fantasy who love witchcraft, magic and a little spookiness. For fans of Daphne du Maurier, Laura Purcell, Michelle Paver and Stacey Halls.

Printed in Great Britain
by Amazon